For Kris —
All ... ...

THE FOUR
WIVES

of the
Sanibel Sunset Detective

It's Your Time

D1512237

MAR. 10/2016

Fiction

Matinee Idol
Foreign Object
Splendido
Magic Man
The Strange
The Sanibel Sunset Detective
The Sanibel Sunset Detective Returns
Another Sanibel Sunset Detective
The Two Sanibel Sunset Detectives
The Hound of the Sanibel Sunset Detective
The Confidence Man

Non-fiction

The Movies of the Eighties (with David Haslam)
If the Other Guy Isn't Jack Nicholson, I've Got the Part
Marquee Guide to Movies on Video
Cuba Portrait of an Island (with Donald Nausbuam)

www.ronbase.com
Read Ron's blog at
www.ronbase.wordpress.com
Contact Ron at
ronbase@ronbase.com

THE FOUR WIVES

of the
Sanibel Sunset Detective

RON BASE

West-End
Books

Library and Archives Canada Cataloguing in Publication
Base, Ron, 1948-, author
        The four wives of the Sanibel sunset detective : a novel
/ Ron Base.
ISBN 978-0-9940645-0-9 (paperback)
        I. Title.
PS8553.A784F69 2015   C813'.54   C2015-907445-2

West-End Books
133 Mill St.
Milton, Ontario
L9T 1S1

Cover design: Jennifer Smith
Text design: Ric Base
Electronic formatting: Ric Base
Sanibel-Captiva map: Ann Kornuta

FIRST EDITION

For Elizabeth, Marilyn, Grace, Anita, and Ursula.
Thank you, ladies.

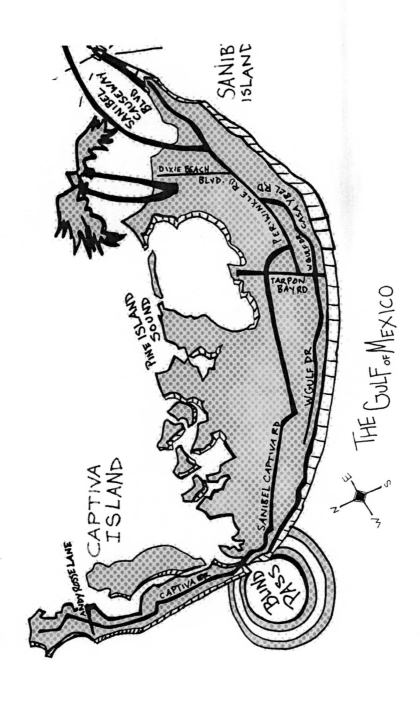

1

Tree Callister and his old friend Rex Baxter were having lunch on the screened-in terrace at the Lighthouse Restaurant, just off Sanibel Island, when Rex said, "I'm getting married in the morning."

"The song from *My Fair Lady* by Lerner and Loewe," Tree said.

"No," Rex said. "I'm getting married in the morning."

"I would argue *My Fair Lady* is the best musical of all time," Tree said. "The blend of story and song in exactly the right measure, the ability of Lerner and Lowe to conjure a Shavian sensibility that echoes the original play without being slavish to it. The inspired, witty score, each song a singular achievement in that once you hear it, you can't stop humming the tune."

Rex looked exasperated. "What's the matter with you? You sound like a bad newspaper critic. This has nothing to do with Lerner and Loewe. I, Rex Baxter, plan to marry tomorrow morning."

Tree looked at him in amazement. "You're getting married?"

"Tomorrow morning," Rex repeated.

"Who are you marrying?"

"Who do you think?"

"My ex-wife?"

"You see?" Rex said. "People underestimate you. Given the opportunity, exercising a little patience, you can figure these things out for yourself."

"You're marrying Kelly. Kelly Fleming."

"You seem to be having trouble with the concept," Rex said.

"You have talked to Kelly about this?"

"I may have floated the idea by her, yes."

"I see," Tree said.

"I'd like you to be my best man," Rex said.

Most of the luncheon diners on the terrace had departed. The marina beyond the restaurant sweltered in the afternoon sun, the lines of yachts, glistening white, unmoving, hardly a stir in the air.

Finally, Tree cleared his throat and eased himself forward, leaning his elbows on the table. "I'm going to be the best man for my best friend who is marrying my ex-wife."

"Do you have a problem with that?" Rex asked.

Tree thought about it for a moment. "No," he said. "I don't suppose I do."

Rex and Tree had been friends, as Rex liked to say, "Ever since the earth cooled," or at least going back to Chicago when Tree was a newspaperman and Rex, a former actor in mostly B pictures, hosted an afternoon movie show on WBBM-TV. This was before Rex became the station's weatherman beloved of all the Chicagoans who ever wanted to know when the next snowstorm would batter the city. By the time Tree, and his wife, Freddie, moved to Sanibel-Captiva, Rex was already embedded in the community, the president of the Chamber of Commerce, once again beloved, and therefore in his element.

It was Rex who had found an office for Tree at the Chamber of Commerce Visitors Center so that Tree could set up The Sanibel Sunset Detective Agency. Rex had lived to regret his altruism. Tree's misadventures as a private eye on Sanibel Island had caused him untold amounts of grief that had, according to Rex, interfered with the thriving tourist trade.

Now Tree supposedly had retired, exhausted, he said, by the constant jeopardy he found himself in on an island where nothing ever happened—except to him. Rex, meantime, had met and fallen in love with a former Chicago newscaster, Kelly Fleming, who, as it happened, was once married to Tree—the second of Tree's four wives.

In fact, Rex had originally introduced Kelly and Tree.

Life certainly could be complicated, Tree mused. Well, he was open-minded about these things, wasn't he? As long as his friend was happy, that's all that counted. Wasn't it?

"This is all happening pretty fast," was all Tree could think to say.

"Not that fast," Rex countered. "I've actually known Kelly longer than you."

"That's true," Tree had to admit.

"Besides, I wanted to get her before she changes her mind."

Rex was kidding, Tree thought. Wasn't he?

A heavyset woman appeared at their table. She focused on Rex. This was not unusual. Rex had been a star television weatherman throughout Heartland America. Sanibel attracted tourists of a certain age from that Heartland, all of whom seemed to recognize their old TV pal.

The woman said in a gentle, breathy voice that Tree immediately recognized, "Rex? Rex Baxter. Is that you?"

Rex gaped in surprise before he said, "Judy? Judy Blair?"

"It's me, Rex," she said with a big smile.

He lumbered to his feet in time for Judy to embrace him. "I thought it was you," she said. "I can't believe it. What are you doing here?"

"Well, for one thing," Rex said, "I'm having lunch with someone you might remember."

She turned and for the first time took a good look at Tree. Her eyes widened. "Tree!"

Now it was Tree's turn to rise awkwardly. Only Judy didn't embrace him. Various emotions played on her smooth, round face—a face Tree barely recognized after all this time. Rex said to Judy, "You don't recognize the guy you married? The father of your children?"

"Yes, of course," Judy said, the warmth in her voice cooling. She mustered a smile. "It's been a long time, Tree."

"Yes," Tree said.

A man appeared behind Judy. Tree had a quick impression of a large, extremely solid fellow with a bull neck, a dramatically-lined face topped by bristling hair he immediately identified as dyed—the male of the species, no matter how prosperous, seemingly incapable of hair coloring that looked at all natural.

Judy turned nervously and said, "Alexei, there you are."

"Yes, I am right here," her companion said. "Would you like to introduce me?"

"My husband, Alexei Markov," Judy said. "Alexei, these are friends from Chicago. Rex Baxter and Tree Callister."

"Good to meet you," Rex said, sticking out his hand.

An attempt had been made to hide the bulk of Alexei Markov beneath a radiant Tommy Bahamas shirt, not tucked in at the waist. The attempt had failed. When he smiled, the dramatic lines of his face softened somewhat and left the impression that behind that rock-hard countenance there lurked the charm that would have attracted Judy. He took Rex's hand in his.

"A pleasure," he said. Then he turned to Tree, and the soft smile was wiped away. "I think you are less a friend, more the ex-husband, am I correct about that?"

"I'm afraid so," Tree said. He was holding out his hand.

Alexei Markov looked at the proffered hand but did not take it. "I have heard so much about you," he said. "None of it very good."

"Alexei, please, that's enough," Judy said in a stricken voice.

Tree took his hand away and looked at Judy. "It's good to see you, Judy."

Judy gave another nervous smile. "Yes, certainly a surprise."

"How long are you here for?" Rex asked.

"We have bought a house here," Alexei Markov said. "We plan to spend much time in this beautiful place."

"I'm the president of the Chamber of Commerce on Sanibel and Captiva," Rex said. "If there's anything I can do to help you settle in, please let me know."

Rex handed Judy one of the business cards he seemed able to produce with a magician's sleight of hand. She took the card and gave a fleeting smile. "That's very kind of you, Rex. You always were so kind."

Tree noticed he was not included in Judy's kindness category.

Markov, demonstrating an equal ability at sleight of hand, plucked the card out of his wife's fingers. "Yes," he agreed. "That is kind of you, Mr. Baxter. We are most appreciative." He looked at his wife. "Judy, I believe we had better have some lunch."

"Good to see you," Judy said to no one in particular.

Markov shot Tree one final, speculative look before taking his wife by the arm and leading her away. Rex watched them disappear into the dining room. "This confirms my suspicion that if you live long enough on this island, you will eventually meet everyone you ever knew from your past life."

"Hard to disagree with you," Tree said.

"Judy didn't seem very happy to see you," Rex said.

"I can't blame her," Tree said. "I wasn't much of a husband."

"You've improved," Rex said. "What's more, it only took you three marriages to do it."

"I'm a slow learner," Tree said.

"That's certainly true," Rex said, getting to his feet. "Just make sure you're at the Island Inn tomorrow morning at eleven."

"You're getting married at the Island Inn?"

"I'll be the guy on the beach with a big smile on his face," Rex said.

"I'm happy for you, Rex," Tree said. "You know that, don't you?"

Rex gave his old friend a skeptical look.

And then he winked.

———————

Why had he married Judy Blair in the first place? Because he was young and Judy was young and slim and in the uncertain, raucous Chicago newspaper world in which he was trying to succeed she represented the stability he had never known? Something like that.

There was something else as well. You were *supposed* to get married and have children. That's what you did; everyone around him was married with kids, all the wild men in the city room eventually left the bars and staggered home to wives. He saw himself as a wild man just like the other boys of the city room so there should be someone waiting when he staggered home. Judy seemed the appropriate candidate for middle-class life. Love? Yeah, sure, he supposed he loved Judy, although during those late nights drinking in places like O'Rourke's or the Billy Goat Tavern, it did cross his mind that wives were to be avoided, not necessarily loved.

Thinking about Judy always saddened him. Not so much Judy as his failure with Judy, and, by extension, with their children. He should have been a better husband and father, but then that's not what he wanted in those days. He wanted to be a reporter; that's all that counted. Everything else, family included, was secondary. Not surprisingly, that wasn't the recipe for a successful marriage. Judy had never forgiven his carelessness—he had never forgiven himself.

Now, all these years later, here she was on Sanibel Island, married to some Russian guy. How did Judy, the quintessential suburban Chicago housewife end up married to a Russian?

Tree decided he wasn't going to think about that, the way he refused to allow himself to think about certain unpleasant realities when he was a young man. He reached his battered old Volkswagen, musing that he was going to have to do something about his beloved Beetle sooner rather than later. The car had served him so well over the years, but having been in police custody in Miami for a time, among the other ills to which he had subjected the car, it was on its last legs.

He opened the dented driver's door. The Beetle uttered a loud, grinding objection, one of many it was issuing lately. He was about to get behind the wheel when he sensed someone and turned with a start to see Alexei Markov coming toward him.

"I thought I might have a word with you in private," Markov said.

Tree now became aware that Markov was not alone. Flanking him was a guy with a brush cut, wearing a golf shirt tight enough to show off a torso that must have been sculpted out of the side of a mountain.

Tree said, "I haven't met your friend, Alexei."

"Valentin is associate of mine," Markov answered.

Valentin looked as though he could tear Tree apart without breathing hard. He also looked as though he would like nothing better than to do just that.

Markov said, "You should know, Mr. Tree Callister, I am not happy to discover you are on this island."

"There is a long line of people who feel the same way you do," Tree said.

"If I had known you were resident here," Markov continued. "I doubt we would have purchased a home."

"You have a bodyguard named Valentin who looks like he just climbed off a pedestal. You should be safe enough," Tree said.

Markov wagged a thick finger under Tree's nose. "Please listen to me, Mr. Callister. I will not say this twice. Here is what you should know about me: I am not someone you wish to anger."

"I am a man of peace," Tree said. "Angering you is the last thing in the world I want to do."

"Stay away from my wife. I know all about you. You are not good person. You are weak and corrupt."

"I'm not sure about the corrupt part," Tree said.

Markov continued, "I understand a mistake a long time ago, but the ripples from that mistake continue to this day. You are despicable human being, and I will take pleasure in making you pay if you come near my wife."

As if to emphasize the point, the sculpted mountainside that was Valentin shifted threateningly closer.

"Come on," Tree said. "Let's get real here. What are you going to do, Valentin? Beat me up in the parking lot? We just met. It's too soon for that."

Valentin frowned. Markov said, "Valentin's English is not so good."

"He will have a chance to improve his language skills here on Sanibel Island," Tree said.

Valentin glowered some more, seeming to take Tree's statement as a personal affront.

"You have been warned," Markov said.

"What have I been warned about?"

"The dark possibilities," Markov said.

Aha, Tree thought. The dark possibilities. Always the dark possibilities.

2

When Freddie got home that night, she and Tree sat outside by the pool, listening to the crowd down at the Mucky Duck make admiring noises as the sun set. Freddie had poured herself the one glass of chardonnay she allowed herself each night—the glass, Tree often mused, she needed in order to steel herself for the news of her husband's latest misadventure.

He waited until she had consumed half the glass before unfolding the day's unlikely tales. First Tree told Freddie about Rex's plan to marry his second wife in the morning. Freddie took the news in stride. She said she had been expecting something like this, although when she had lunch with Kelly a week ago, the former Chicago news anchor seemed distracted and not all that happy.

"You had lunch with Kelly?" said a surprised Tree.

"A quick bite," Freddie said.

"You didn't tell me," Tree said.

"I guess with all I've got on my plate at the moment, it must have slipped my mind," Freddie said.

"You have a lot on your plate?"

"Busy with work," she said vaguely.

Then he told Freddie about his encounter with Judy, his first wife. "I don't think I've ever met Judy," Freddie said.

"I haven't spoken to her in years," Tree said. "Even when the kids were in trouble, she never called me."

"But then you never called her, did you?"

Tree ignored this. "When she showed up at the Lighthouse this afternoon, I barely recognized her, and I don't think she recognized me. But she didn't miss Rex, of course."

"What is she doing here?"

"She and her husband bought a home on the island. He's a Russian guy. Alexei Markov. Unless I'm mistaken, he threatened me."

"I'm sure you're exaggerating."

"He probably wouldn't do anything himself. He would probably get Valentin to do it."

"Who is Valentin?"

"Alexei's bodyguard. He looks like a killing machine hacked out of marble by Michelangelo."

"You're sure you're not making this up?" Freddie questioned.

"Scout's honor," Tree said.

"And this was after your best friend told you he was going to marry your second wife."

"There's never a dull moment," Tree said.

"That's for sure," Freddie said, taking a sip of her wine.

It was the greatest embarrassment of Tree's life—a life filled with embarrassments—that he had been married four times. He reconciled this with the argument that he had to experience three wives before he got to the wife who really counted, Fredryka Stayner, known to everyone as Freddie.

They had met in Chicago, Freddie the poised, elegantly beautiful vice president of a major food chain, Tree the rumpled, hard-drinking newspaperman. Well, sort of rumpled; he had made himself fairly presentable for the Gold Coast dinner party where he had been introduced to Freddie. And he was not all that hard drinking by the time he met her. After they became a couple, it didn't seem necessary to ever have a drink again, and so he stopped, about the time the *Sun-Times* downsized him, thus bringing to an abrupt end the career that had been his life.

By then, Freddie had become fed up with the constant demands of her job and, to everyone's surprise, decided to take a position running Dayton's on Sanibel Island, the flagship of a small chain of supermarkets located along Florida's west coast.

Tree and Freddie had found a home on Andy Rosse Lane on the neighboring island of Captiva.

Lacking much to do with himself, Tree in a moment of madness, having spent much of his life snooping into other people's lives, decided to become a private investigator. The Sanibel Sunset Detective Agency was a terrible mistake, everyone thought. Even supportive Freddie wondered at her husband's sanity. Eventually, after being shot—shot twice in fact—Tree had decided that everyone may have been right, and maybe he should get out of the detective business. Thus, the fired Chicago newspaperman was now a retired Sanibel Sunset detective.

That, as Freddie and Rex were quick to point out, had not stopped him from getting into hot water. The threatening Russian husband of Tree's first wife was the latest evidence of that.

"I don't think I was that bad a husband," Tree said.

Freddie said, "Okay," in a non-committal voice.

Tree looked at her. "This is the part where you are supposed to say, 'Oh, darling, you're such a wonderful husband, you couldn't possibly have been that bad.'"

"You are a—mostly—wonderful husband," Freddie said. "Particularly when you stay out of trouble. But obviously Judy has a different view of your relationship, and she appears to have shared that view with her new husband."

"It's hard to believe," Tree said. "Judy was a quiet, conservative woman from the Chicago suburbs who wanted nothing more than to be a stay-at-home mom back in the days when they were simply called housewives. How did she ever manage to end up marrying some Russian thug?"

"A rich Russian thug by the sound of things," Freddie said.

"How rich do Russians have to be to have bodyguards?"

"Pretty rich, I would imagine," Freddie said.

Tree wondered what had turned him from a "bad" husband into a "good" one. Or perhaps using the word "good" in connection with him was going too far. More accurate to say he had been transformed into a "better" husband. What had brought that about? Age? Yes, that was part of it.

But more than anything, he decided, it was Freddie. And that created another unanswerable question. What was it about one person whom you supposedly loved but treated badly, as opposed to another you also loved but it would never cross your mind to mistreat? Each time he looked at Freddie, he felt unconditional love that ten years of marriage had failed to dampen.

How was that?

"What are you thinking?" Freddie said, interrupting his reverie. "I seem to have lost you."

"I was thinking about how much I love you."

"You weren't thinking that three of your wives are now living on one little island and that it might be getting a titch crowded?"

"A titch?" said Tree.

"A titch," affirmed Freddie.

"How do you feel about it?"

"There is not much either of us can do about it." She grinned. "Except for one thing."

"What's that?"

"Get ready for your ex-wife's wedding."

———————

Tree rolled around restlessly, unable to sleep. He thought about Judy and the path that would have taken her to Alexei Markov. Finally, his curiosity got the better of him. He got up and padded out of the bedroom into the office where he sat at his laptop and Googled Alexei Markov.

A farmer's son, according to Google, Markov had been born in a town called Borisov in Belarus in 1950. Forbes estimated his wealth at two billion dollars, placing him in the lower ranks of the so-called oligarchs who had amassed fortunes following perestroika.

Markov's millions were mostly accumulated after he got into the fertilizer business during the Boris Yeltsin era. This was when things began to loosen up and he could take advantage of corrupt government officials as he formed a company that became Russia's largest producer of potassium fertilizers.

He had sold his interest in the company the year before, amid allegations from Canadian officials that it was a front for international arms dealers who needed to launder money and were able to do it through Markov. Canada had gone so far as to deny him entry.

Markov seemed to have no trouble getting into the United States, despite the U.S. government's recent crackdown on wealthy Russians. He had been married twice. His first wife was a well-known Russian model. He was said to have a number of mistresses, most notably, the Norwegian actress, Elin Danielsen. He easily found a photograph of Danielsen. Lots of them. High cheekbones. Impressive breasts. However, there was nothing on the Internet about Markov marrying a quiet former Chicago housewife named Judy Conroy.

Perhaps she lacked the cheekbones.

3

Overcast skies threatened more of the rain that had been falling on and off for the past week. The small number of guests invited to the wedding of Kelly Fleming and Rex Baxter gathered on the beach at the Island Inn, seated on folding chairs in front of a podium draped in white chiffon. The groom waited nearby, tall and debonair in a dark suit and bright yellow tie, shaved and shining, suitably nervous, but trying not to show it.

Sanibel Island's mayor was there along with the county commissioner, the president of the Fort Myers Chamber of Commerce, and the mayor of Fort Myers Beach. Todd Jackson was present, elegantly pressed as usual. He operated Sanibel Biohazard, a company that specialized in crime scene cleanups. He and Rex had been friends from the time Rex first arrived on the island. With Todd was his wife, Candace, who happened to be a notary public and thus authorized to marry the bride and groom.

Freddie glowed in a Stella Jean dress, blazing with orange and crimson triangles. Tree stood beside Rex wearing the blue blazer and striped tie he usually reserved for court appearances. The wind picked up slightly. Tree could see white-capped waves slapping against the shore beyond the undergrowth that formed a line of defense along this part of the beach.

Tree said to Rex, "How are you doing?"

"It's not every day I get married," Rex answered.

"How long have you been single?"

"Thirty years, maybe longer," Rex said.

"That long," was all Tree could think to say.

"You're not doing very well at the small talk," Rex said.

"Give me a break," said Tree. "It's not often my best friend marries my ex-wife."

Rex looked at his watch.

Freddie motioned to Tree. He excused himself from Rex and walked over to where she was standing. She whispered in his ear: "Shouldn't the bride be here by now? It's after eleven."

"Kelly likes to be fashionably late," Tree said. "That way she can make an entrance."

"Who's giving Kelly away?" Freddie asked.

"Are you kidding? No one gives Kelly away."

Tree went back to Rex who said, "She was late for your wedding, too."

"I don't remember," Tree said.

"I do," Rex replied. "I was the best man."

"You've been my best man at all my weddings."

"Not the first one," Rex said. "That was before my time."

"Judy was about thirty pounds lighter, and she hadn't met any Russians," Tree said.

"Ain't that a kick?" Rex said.

"I'm not sure that's how I would describe it," Tree said.

"There are a whole lot of people I would have picked to end up with a rich Russian before I got to Judy," Rex said.

"You know he's rich?"

"I know everyone who's rich on the island," Rex said.

Kelly chose that moment to make her entrance. She wore a short white dress and a grim expression. She ignored the scattered applause that greeted her, walking straight over to Tree and Rex.

"I'm sorry," she said to Rex. "I can't do this. I can't."

Then she turned on her heel and marched back off the beach, leaving behind her a stunned silence. None of the guests turned to view Kelly's departure. Everyone stared resolutely forward.

For a couple of moments, Rex seemed frozen in place as though the news of what had just happened failed to reach his brain. Then he straightened, the indication his brain had finally kicked in and was now trying to process fast-moving events. "That's not a good start to our marriage," he said in a choked voice.

"Let me talk to her," Tree said. And before Rex or anyone else could object, he dashed after Kelly.

He caught up with her just off the beach in the parking lot. Her back was to him. Her straight back, smartly sheathed in white, he couldn't help but notice, slim hips molded into the linen skirt. She was handing her ticket to a parking attendant. As the attendant went to get her car, she turned to Tree, no hint of emotion showing on the shimmering face of the woman he briefly loved in another lifetime, and who in that lifetime was Chicago's most famous newscaster. That had been an unpromising combination: bright, vivacious television personality matched with beaten up *Sun-Times* reporter. Somehow it didn't go together. Not even close. Kelly had departed quickly, brusquely, probably showing about the same level of emotion she was showing now.

She nodded in the direction of the attendant. "He's getting my car." As if that needed explanation.

"Don't do this," Tree said.

"I need my car," Kelly said.

"Please, Kelly."

"He sent you." She added her own note of surprise to the announcement.

"Nobody sent me," Tree said. "Everyone's too stunned to speak."

"Everyone except you, Tree. Everyone except my former husband who's used to women walking out on him."

"At least I got you to the altar," Tree said.

"And wasn't that a mistake—not one I'm going to repeat."

"You might have told Rex before today."

"Yes, well, I feel badly about that. Look it's a mess. Things have happened."

"What kinds of things?"

"Things I thought I'd gotten past. But it turns out I haven't. It doesn't matter at this point," she said. "It's too late."

"No, it isn't, Kelly," Tree said. "You can come back. Everyone will understand. Last minute jitters, that's all."

She shook her head. "No, this is better than the two of us married, and me seething with resentment."

"You're seething with resentment?"

"Not at this moment, no. But it wouldn't be long in coming, believe me."

"Whatever's gone on, this is no way to handle it."

"I'm well aware of that," she said. "But I'm not going back there. I'm sorry, but I'm not."

The attendant had returned with her car, a featureless white Ford Taurus, like a million others strewn across South Florida parking lots. Not the kind of car, Tree reflected, Kelly would ever have been found dead in when he was married to her. The attendant got out and held the door for her.

"So what are you going to do?"

"You mean what am I going to do if I'm not getting married this morning? I don't know, Tree. I have no idea. I need time to think."

"I don't understand what's happened," Tree said helplessly.

She paused getting into her car. "Didn't you ever try something just because you were intrigued, only to find out it wasn't for you? Then you pay a big price for your little experiment, and it hangs over you and refuses to go away."

Tree just stood there as she handed the attendant a folded bill. Then she was in the car and driving away, out onto West Gulf Drive. He continued to stand there, numb with disbelief, a pillar of salt.

His cellphone began to vibrate in his pocket. For a wild moment he thought it might be Kelly calling him from the car. But it wasn't Kelly.

"Tree," a voice said, "it's Patricia Laine."

Tree blanked. "Patricia?"

"Pat. Pat Laine. Remember me?"

He gulped, "Pat."

"We used to be married. Remember?"

"Where are you?"

"Where am I?"

"Yes," he said. "Where are you?"

"Right at this moment, I'm in jail," she said.

4

The Palm Beach County Sheriff's Office Central Detention Center was spread over seventeen flat arid acres off Fairgrounds Road in suburban West Palm Beach, a massive gray cage incongruous against the cloudless blue of the Florida sky. Tree wondered where they found all the prisoners to put into these places, but the state of Florida seemed to have no trouble filling them.

The facility, according to its website, currently housed nine-hundred eighty-eight inmates. The nine-hundred eighty-ninth was waiting outside the jail wearing a silver evening gown, clutching at a beaten brown leather shoulder bag that didn't go with her dress. Tree stopped to stare. Of course. How else would Patricia Laine be dressed in front of a jail?

Every guy in the *Sun-Times* newsroom had loved Pat. No one could resist her. Armies of men trailed after her. Before Tree met her, he heard about the hearts she had left broken around the Chicago newspaper world. How had he ever thought she wouldn't break his heart? That was the mystery, wasn't it? You never think it's going to happen to you. As good an explanation as any, Tree supposed.

She had started modeling as a teenager in Los Angeles, wore a bikini in a low budget horror movie before getting into local television. When Tree met her, she had followed a husband to Chicago, dumped him, and then did some more modeling before somehow managing to work herself into the editorship of what they used to call "the women's section" of the *Sun-Times*.

How Pat ever got that job mystified Tree, except as he got to know her better, it really didn't. Whatever Pat did, she did with tremendous style, and she had that ability to simultaneously flirt with and manipulate the men who invariably were suckers for her, Tree included. The difference was that he and Pat had ended up marrying one another. How had that happened? By the time Tree figured out that it was a mistake, Pat was headed for the exit accompanied by one of the paper's senior editors—the guy who had hired her in the first place.

Too late, Tree understood why.

Since their divorce, Tree had not heard a word from her. For all he had known, she was still in Chicago, although no longer with the *Sun-Times*. That had ended in pretty short order when she ran off with the editor.

He knew now that Pat wasn't in Chicago. Here she was in a silver evening gown outside the Palm Beach Detention Center, coming toward him, balancing precariously on high heels, silvery to match her dress. She was very much as he remembered her, more lines on her face, of course, but still long and lithe, hair cut shorter than before, not quite reaching her shoulders.

"My God, Tree, look at you; you got old," she said just before she rushed into his arms and hugged him.

"You've hardly changed at all," he said, the first line of dialogue he had spoken to her in—what?—twenty-five years? Not exactly Bogart and Bergman in *Casablanca*, but the best he could do on short notice.

"*Gawd*! I must look an awful mess," Pat exclaimed. No sooner had she hugged him than she pulled away, as though he was electrified and she had just received a shock. A quick up and down inspection followed. "You always were such an awful dresser. Nothing's changed. You still look as though you slept in your clothes. You really should do something about that shirt." She looked at her watch. "We don't have much time."

He looked at her in astonishment. "Time for what?"

"Where are you parked?"

"Across the street, but listen to me, Pat—"

"Okay, the first thing you should know, I'm not called Pat anymore."

"What do they call you?"

"I'm called Skye. That's with an *e*. Skye Blair."

"Look, Skye or Pat or whatever you're being called today, let's take a moment here."

"We don't have a moment. We have to get over to the convention center."

"What convention center? What are you talking about?" Tree's head was spinning.

"What do you mean, what convention center? The West Palm Beach Convention Center. What convention center do you think I'm talking about? That's where they're holding the Art and Antique Show."

"Pat, you just got out of jail."

"Skye. I told you I am now Skye."

"Either way, I've driven across Florida because you said you needed help."

"I do need help. I need a drive to the convention center."

"I'm not driving you anywhere. Not until you tell me what's going on here."

She stopped long enough to heave a dramatic sigh. "All right, Tree. Fine. You always did want to have it your way. What is it you want to know?"

"Let's start with what you were doing in jail."

"It's entrapment, pure and simple. That's why I have to get to the convention center."

"Entrapment? What kind of entrapment?"

"The kind that traps you, the kind that causes you to end up in prison, that kind. Now can we go to the convention center?"

"Why? What's going on at the convention center?"

Pat looked at him like he was crazy. "I told you what's going on. The Art and Antique Show, that's what's going on."

"You have to get to an antiques show?"

"Honestly, Tree. You always were a little dense. I used to wonder how you were ever a journalist. Don't get your shirt in a knot. I'm kidding. Sort of. Half kidding."

"Pat."

"Because that's where I'm meeting Tal, that's why." As though any moron should know that.

"I'm missing something here," Tree said. "Who is Tal?"

"Tal. Tal Fiala. He's my lawyer. Where did you say your car was?"

"It's across the street. But Pat, er, Skye, I need you to tell me why you're in trouble..."

But she wasn't listening, already headed across the roadway. "Come on," she called back to him. "We don't have a lot of time to waste."

She reached the parking lot and stopped dead when she saw the Beetle. "Tree, tell me this isn't your car. Please, reassure me you're not driving this thing."

He caught up with her and said, "I'm afraid it is."

"Tree, I can't drive up to the Palm Beach Convention Center in that thing. I can't. What will people think?"

"Pat, you just got out of jail."

"Hey, it's Palm Beach. Everyone knows someone who's been in jail. But this car, that's something else entirely. People will talk."

"You've got a choice," Tree said opening the driver's side door. "Either you can come with me. Or you can call one of your Palm Beach friends with a better car."

"You're such a bastard, you know that, Tree? You've always been a bastard. Really, you have. I'm kidding. Sort of. Half kidding."

He closed the door and started the Beetle's engine. She stamped her feet a couple of times, and made loud sounds of irritation and then flounced around and got in the car.

"I hate you, you know," she said. "I've always hated you. Why we ever got married, I'll never know. I can't even remember at this point. You got me drunk, that's what must have happened."

"Pat," Tree sighed.

"Call me Skye," Pat said.

———

As they drove to the convention center, Pat—or Skye—announced, "It's a conspiracy. Pure and simple. They are out to get me."

"Who's out to get you?" Tree asked.

"Who do you think? The police. The Palm Beach district attorney."

"Pat, I want you to stop this. I can't help you if you won't tell me what they arrested you for."

"It's Skye, I told you it's Skye." Her voice trembled.

"Stop it. I married Patricia Laine. You're still Patricia to me."

"And who says I was arrested?"

"You were standing outside the Palm Beach jail."

"It was awful, just so awful." Her voice trembled more. A tear ran down her cheek. "I've never been so humiliated."

"Tell me what happened."

"It's all a misunderstanding. I never stole anything." As soon as those words were out, the waterworks started. Pat buried her face against tiny fists, and sobbed loudly.

Tree reached out and touched her shoulder. "Pat," he said gently. "Tell me what happened. What do they say you stole?"

She lifted her face up. It was stained with tears. "They're saying I stole money from Doris."

"Who is Doris?"

The question inspired a further burst of tears. "She's an old friend, a very old friend. Doris Bermann. I've known her forever."

"Why do they think you took her money?"

"I—I have power of attorney over Doris's affairs. They say I took money from her bank account. That's a lie. I never did any such thing."

"What does Doris have to say about all this?"

"She doesn't say anything. She suffers from dementia. She knew she was in trouble a year ago. Losing her memory. It was getting really bad, and she had to do something. She trusted me. I am her friend."

"So she gave you power of attorney so you could handle her affairs."

Pat nodded eagerly, as though Tree had finally understood a particularly difficult algebra problem. "Yes, yes. That's right. It was all above board. It was what Doris wanted. She was ill. There was no one else but me. I would never hurt her."

"How much do they say you stole?"

"Don't use that word, stole," she snapped. "I hate that word. I never stole a single thing. I'm her friend. Friends can't steal from one another. It's not like I broke into her house or something. It was all above board, like I said."

"How much, Pat?"

"I wish you wouldn't call me Pat," she said amid more tears. "I hate that name. I've changed. So much has changed. I'm evolving. Growing. I'm not the person I used to be. I'm Skye now."

"How much?"

"I don't know what difference the money makes. It's all so ridiculous. It's a rush to judgment, I'm telling you that, Tree. They are out to get me, I swear they are. It's the American justice system. It's relentless, unforgiving. You know we have more people in jail here than they do in China? Do you know that?"

"Pat!"

"All right, all right. They're saying five million dollars."

"You stole five million dollars?"

"No, I didn't. That's what they're saying, but it's not true. None of it's true."

5

A six-foot-nine-inch oxidized green bronze of a Civil War infantryman frowned at Tree in the main entrance foyer. Pan, Greek god of the wild, pipes in hand, was also cast in bronze, a devilish grin inviting sybaritic activities Tree had no time for this afternoon as he hurried to keep up with Pat.

The woman who had seemed so out of place outside a prison in a silver evening gown appeared right at home in the under-lit maze of the Palm Beach Jewelry, Art and Antique Show, threading her way through an upscale crowd not in evening attire but not giving a second look to a woman who was. Tree brushed past a middle-aged woman holding up a jewel for inspection. "What about the sapphire?" she called to a white-haired man. "Oh, go ahead," said the white-haired man, as though buying a sapphire was something he did most days.

A hollow-eyed marble Caesar peered sightlessly at him. French legionnaires in bright red trousers, captured in oils, stood forever at attention closely watched by a fluffy dog. Neatly pressed little girls swore never to smoke cigars during prayers in the inked panels of Ronald Searle's quirky cartoons. A happy lad in a sailor's hat posed at the wheel of a yacht with his pipe-smoking Dad for a *Saturday Evening Post* cover declaring the normalcy of a generation of white bread Americans.

Pat came abruptly to a stop, Tree nearly crashing into her. She had magically produced a cellphone, pressing it against her ear, her expression tense with concern. "I'm here," she stated. "What? Here. At the convention center. Where are you?" She paused to listen to what was being said on the other end of the line. "Stay where you are. I'm coming to you."

And without so much as a glance at Tree, she was off again, turning past a glass display case of antique urns, pushing her way through the crowd and then making a left along a shadowy corridor full of purses and jewelry. Finally, she burst onto a wide thoroughfare devoted to Impressionist wannabes preoccupied with Parisian street scenes.

She turned another corner and was confronted by a tall man with streaked gray hair wearing a shirt decorated with multi-colored ferns. The tall man stood beside an oil painting of a two-fisted hombre in a fedora poised over a half-naked blonde, while behind the hombre a guy in a bow tie burst through the door.

Pat threw herself against the shirt of ferns. "Oh, Tal," she said. "It's so horrible."

Tal Fiala put a tentative arm around her, glancing at Tree as he did. "It's all right, pet," he said in an uncertain voice. "It's going to be all right now."

She looked up at him longingly. He looked nervous. He said, "Are you familiar with the work of James Alfred Meese?"

"Tal, what happened? You said you would be at the jail when they released me." Pat, shifting into the accusatory mode to which Tree had been subjected many times, accompanied by more of the longing looks he had not seen for a long time.

"Miscommunication, pet," Tal pronounced. "The curse of modern society, even in this age of technological marvels. I was certain the district attorney's office said you were to be released this afternoon."

"How could they have told you that? I told you I was getting out late this morning. You said you would be there." Pat had disengaged herself from him and now the longing look was replaced by one that was more familiar to Tree: demanding.

"Take a look at this work," Tal said, shifting his attention back to the painting. "Meese was an illustrator of the highest caliber, trapped in a lowbrow business that required him to squander his talent producing countless covers for the so-called pulp fiction paperbacks published in the fifties. Nonetheless, laboring against great odds, he was still able to create highly erotic, original work." He looked at Tree. "Are you a fan of pulp-fiction art, my friend?"

"Not really," Tree said, thinking his life was pulp fiction. "But I used to be married to Pat."

"Then you must be Robert Bronsky."

"No, I believe he was my successor. Well, I don't believe he was my successor, he was my successor."

"I don't want to hear about Bobby," Pat said in a cross voice. "That's water under a bridge."

"Then if you're not the regrettable Mr. Bronsky, who are you?"

"Tree Callister. More water under the bridge."

"Tree Canister?" Tal appeared perplexed. He said to Pat, "Were you married to a Tree Canister?"

"Callister," Tree said.

"I told you about Tree," Pat said. "I'm sure I did."

"So many husbands and lovers, pet. It's hard to keep track." He fixed friendly eyes on Tree. "Tree, it's—well, I suppose under the circumstances it's hardly a pleasure to meet you. But good that you're here to help Skye, even if I have never heard of you."

"That's not true," Pat protested.

"Tree." Tal said it as if he had encountered a previously unknown word requiring practice to pronounce properly. "Tree. You would think if I heard that name attached to a former husband I would remember it."

"It was a short marriage," Tree said.

Tal gave him a look, part speculation, Tree thought, part jealousy. "And yet here you are, the growing tree, the spreading tree, the knight to the rescue."

"When I couldn't get in touch with you, I called Tree," Pat said. "It's a good thing I did. I was stranded outside that jail in an evening gown."

"Yes, most fortunate." Tal said this in such a way as to suggest it wasn't all that fortunate.

Pat gave him a nasty look. He ignored it in favor of more study of the two-fisted guy in the fedora with the half-naked blonde. "I collect Meese's works," Tal said. "Unfortunately, where this particular piece is concerned, my friend Morton is demanding what amounts to highway robbery."

As if by magic, a gnome-like man with a bald head and rimless glasses appeared, scowling. "Morty," there you are," said Tal Fiala. "I was just saying nasty things about you."

"It's not highway robbery," Morton protested. "It's fair market value for Meese's work."

"I have offered Morty five thousand for the work," Tal Fiala said.

"It's an insult," Morton said.

"It's a good offer," said Tal. "You should take it."

"Over my dead body," Morton said.

"Yes, well, don't tempt me, Morty. Don't tempt me." Tal waved a dismissive hand in Morton's direction and resumed his inspection of Tree. "Now for the unknown husband. While I'm fascinated to meet a previously hidden mistake of Skye's, and while I do appreciate you delivering her here, forgive me Mr. Tree Canister..."

"Callister," Tree corrected.

"Tree is a private detective." Pat said it in a way that suggested this was a very important thing to be.

Tal did not seem impressed. "Is he now?" he said, dryly. "A detective named Tree. Wonders never do cease, do they?"

"Tree is going to prove our innocence."

"No, I'm not." Tree couldn't keep the look of shock off his face. "That's not what I'm here for."

"Then what are you here for?" Tal demanded.

"What's this about 'our' innocence?" Tree addressed Pat. "Are you both involved in this?"

"It's like I told you, Tal is my attorney."

"A terrible mistake," added Tal. "All of it. That will become apparent as soon as the details of the case are revealed. I am mounting a strong defense. The local authorities will be very sorry they tried to frame Skye."

"Good," Tree said. "Then you won't be needing me."

"You said you'd help us," Pat said in a reproachful voice.

"I never said any such thing," Tree said.

"We won't be needing help, pet."

"They put me in jail, Tal. You were nowhere to be seen. Tree at least was there for me when I needed him."

That caused a frown to crease Tal's otherwise resolutely pleasant features. "I have already explained to you what happened. Miscommunication. Adding Mr. Canister to the mix, I fear we won't be able to see the forest for the tree," Tal said, pleased with his joke. "Our growing tree will just complicate an already overly complicated situation."

"I want him to help us," Pat said insistently.

"There's nothing I can do for you," Tree said.

"Exactly," Tal said. "Go away little tree. Grow somewhere else."

Morton reappeared, as if out of a puff of smoke. "Tell you what," he said to Tal Fiala, "because I'm a nice guy, you write me a check right here and now for five thousand, five hundred dollars, and the Meese is yours."

"Done!" exclaimed Tal, victorious.

Tree looked at the two-fisted guy in the fedora. Could the half-naked blonde be the fedora guy's ex-wife? That might explain the fists.

6

By the time Tree got home that night, the traffic had thinned along Sanibel-Captiva Road, and the crowds, having watched the sun set at the Mucky Duck, had drifted off Andy Rosse Lane. A familiar black Cadillac Escalade was parked beside Freddie's Mercedes, giving the impression the rich lived here. Tree parked the Beetle, evidence that they didn't.

Rex Baxter lay on the sofa in the living room, snoring softly. He wore jeans and a white dress shirt. Tree noticed specs of crimson on Rex's shirtsleeve. He found Freddie in shorts on the terrace, a glass of chardonnay in hand. "This is my second," she announced after he kissed her mouth. "I figure I deserve it, what with my husband off to see his third ex-wife while his friend nurses a broken heart brought on by my husband's second ex-wife. Or do I have the order wrong?"

"Nope," said Tree. "You've got them in the proper order. Was Rex drunk when he got here?"

"No, just broken-hearted and exhausted from lack of sleep. I told him to stretch out on the sofa. He's been there ever since, poor soul."

"No word from Kelly?"

Freddie shook her head. "You were expecting her to get in touch?"

"I don't know. I'm past knowing what to expect where wives are concerned."

"Which brings us to the subject of Wife Number Three. How did it go with her?"

Tree rolled his eyes. "I've spent a fair amount of time this afternoon wondering what I did to deserve this."

"You married too many women," Freddie said.

"Ah, that's what it is," Tree said.

"My suggestion is you don't marry any more," Freddie said.

"Best advice I've had all day," Tree said.

As quickly as he could, he filled Freddie in on what had happened in Palm Beach: meeting Patricia outside the local jail, her insistence on calling herself Skye, the revelation she had been charged with defrauding a rich widow suffering from dementia, the trip to the convention center where he met her lawyer, Tal Fiala."

"What did you do?" Freddie asked once he had finished.

"I told her I was retired from the private investigation business," Tree said.

"You're the only one who seems to think so."

"I said that I was sorry, but there was nothing I could do for her."

"How did Patricia—or Skye—react?"

"It was more Tal Fiala's reaction. He was adamant he didn't need help from an ex-husband he didn't even know existed."

"What about Pat?"

"She called me a lot of names and said it was my fault that the marriage broke up."

"And is that an accurate assessment, do you think?"

"I don't know. I suppose it is, although there is a possibility we both might have contributed. The marriage certainly wasn't helped when she moved in with my editor."

"The four wives of the Sanibel Sunset Detective," Freddie said. It didn't sound all that great to Tree's ears. But at least she said it with a smile.

That was a smile, wasn't it?

"What can I tell you? Just when I thought I had gotten away, my mistakes have come back to haunt me."

"Not to complicate your life any more than it is," Freddie said.

Tree groaned. "Has it got to do with wives?"

"Something to do with this wife, I'm afraid."

"You?"

"Me. A dispute at work. Maybe. I stress that word maybe."

"A dispute? Over what?"

"Over the way things are being done, differing views on what's being done, and, I suppose, about what's not being done," Freddie answered enigmatically. "Like I say, maybe. For now it's maybe. But it's why I'm going to have a third glass of wine."

Before Tree could probe further, he was stopped by a sound from the other room: Rex stirring.

Freddie said, "Let's just keep this to ourselves for now," a moment before Rex appeared looking sleepy and holding his Blackberry. His white shirt hung out of his jeans.

"I fell asleep," he said.

"That's all right," Tree said.

"Can I get you something?" Freddie said. "Something to drink?"

"No, thanks," Rex said. He appeared distracted, looking down at his Blackberry. After a moment, he ceased his fiddling with the phone and went over and sat down near Freddie. She said, "You sure you wouldn't like a glass of wine, Rex?"

"I shouldn't be drinking right now, given everything that's happened. I've got to keep a clear head. That's important, right now."

Tree gave his friend a worried look. "Are you all right?"

Rex's eyes looked hollow. They scared Tree. "No, I'm not all right, if you want to know the truth. I've really screwed things up. I've screwed up, and I'm sitting here and I don't know how to get out of it."

Freddie and Tree traded glances. Freddie reached across to put her hand gently on Rex's hand. "You've been through a lot. It's going to take time to get over this. Don't beat yourself up."

To Tree's surprise, he saw a tear roll down Rex's cheek. In all the years he had known him, he had never seen his friend cry.

"This is a mess," Rex said. "This is a terrible, awful mess."

"How about something to eat?" Freddie said, voicing her innate belief that any crisis could be resolved with a good meal. "We can all have some dinner."

"I'm not hungry," Rex said. He lifted his phone to eye level, squinting at it as though having trouble seeing it properly. Then he sighed and put the phone on the table, lowering his head as if bowing to the gods of fate.

The sound of the front door chimes rang through the house. Rex's head jerked up in alarm. Tree said, "Someone at the door, that's all. I'll get it."

"I don't want to talk to anyone right now," Rex said.

Tree went up into the living room and crossed to the entrance door. When he opened it he found Detective Cee Jay Boone standing on the threshold. His initial impression of the African American police officer, who, in the course of their relationship, had served as both occasional ally and dedicated foe, was that she had lost even more weight since the last time he saw her. Was that a hint of gray threaded through her close-cropped hair? Time was passing. Age was catching up with both of them, Tree mused.

Right behind Cee Jay was her partner, Detective Owen Markfield. No gray in his hair, no sense that age was the enemy attacking his neatly layered blond highlights. He remained the incarnation of Sanibel's resident beach boy detective, smoothly tanned and camera-ready for the TV series in which he would never star. Just as well, since Markfield undoubtedly would cast Tree in the recurring role of villain. As the result of a previous nasty encounter, Markfield had sworn to "get him". So far, the detective had failed, but certainly not for lack of trying.

Cee Jay, as she usually did when appearing at Tree's house, looked grim. It was, Tree noted, hard for Markfield to keep the smirk off his face.

"Tree," Cee Jay said.

"Detective Boone, what brings you out here at this time of night?"

"I am looking for Rex Baxter."

"Why are you looking for him, Detective?"

"I have an arrest warrant for him."

Tree felt his stomach tighten. "For what?"

"Is he here or not?" Cee Jay demanded.

Rex materialized behind Tree, pale and tense. "I'm here," he said. "What is it you want?"

"Rex Baxter," Cee Jay said in a formal voice. "You are under arrest."

Tree looked at her in astonishment. "What's the charge?"

"We are charging Mr. Baxter with the murder of Kelly Fleming," Cee Jay announced.

7

T. Emmett Hawkins, he of the bow tie and the silky Southern manners, was considered the best criminal lawyer on the Florida's west coast. Tree had had a number of dealings with him over the years, not all of them good. Right now, however, resplendent in his book-lined Fort Myers office, perched on a worn leather armchair, Hawkins looked like the man for the job of defending Rex. He exuded the necessary air of discreet authority, a gentleman who would succeed, even if it meant kicking the daylights out of an opponent in a back alley—as long as it didn't dirty his manicured nails.

Hawkins said, "Sooner or later, the prosecution must disclose its case to us but, from what I can gather so far, they believe that after Ms. Fleming abandoned Rex at the wedding, she returned to his house to gather up her things, and that is when she died of what they are calling blunt-force trauma, suffered when she was struck on the head by a firm object, wielded, they say, by Rex."

"What kind of object?" Tree asked.

"The prosecution so far isn't saying," Hawkins replied. "Rex then placed the body in a pool storage area. The body was discovered by the young woman who regularly cleans the pool and who uses the pool-house facility to store equipment. The police arrived around four o'clock, and by eight had decided Rex was their man and started to look for him."

"And arrested him at our place," Freddie said.

"That is correct," agreed Hawkins.

The endless media barrage over the past few days, the hours of speculation on cable television news, had lent a surreal air to Kelly's death and Rex's arrest. Tree was having a hard time associating any of this with the woman to whom he was once married. The reality of his former wife's death had sunk in, he told himself, except it hadn't.

He was hearing about people he had known intimately, and yet he did not know these people at all. They were somehow reduced to characters in a bad tabloid story—the kind of cliché-filled exploitation he had tried to steer clear of as a reporter, but which now fed the voracious demands of the twenty-four hour-television news cycle.

"What are the chances you can get Rex out on bail?" Freddie asked.

Hawkins lifted his slim shoulders up and down in his restrained version of a shrug. "You probably know the answer to that question as well as I," he said. "Given the nature of the charges on the one hand, and the high profile of this case, I would say not good. On the other hand, Rex is a pillar of the Sanibel-Captiva community with no criminal record and a very low flight risk. So we shall see."

"Cable television is reporting they found Kelly's blood on Rex's clothing," Freddie said.

Hawkins raised his soft white hands and made them flutter dismissively on either side of his soft white face. "According to Rex, she cut her finger when she came back to the house to collect her things. He helped her with a Band-Aid, which is when he got her blood on his shirt."

Hawkins returned his hands to the landing strip formed by the chair's armrests. The hands, Tree noticed, lay at rest, like two exhausted doves.

"I don't believe it," Tree said.

Hawkins turned his gaze toward Tree, studying him from beneath heavily-lidded eyes. "You do not believe Rex helped your ex-wife after she cut her finger?"

"I don't believe my best friend killed my former wife in a fit of rage."

"Good," Hawkins said, accompanying the word with a tiny smile. "The fact that you believe in his innocence will help us enormously in reaching a satisfactory outcome to this whole sad affair."

"How will that help?" Freddie asked.

Hawkins addressed Freddie. "If Rex did not kill his fiancée—and I join with Tree here in believing he didn't—then that means the person who did kill her is still out there. I have pointed out to Tree in the past that the fastest way to prove a person's innocence is to discover the guilty party."

Freddie looked at Tree. "I guess the question is, who would want to murder Kelly?"

"There is one other possible suspect, I suppose," Tree said. "Someone who was jealous, who didn't want her marrying Rex."

"And who would that be?" inquired Hawkins.

"Me," Tree said.

Freddie navigated the Mercedes along McGregor Boulevard. Tree slumped beside her in the passenger seat. "How are you feeling?" Freddie asked.

"Numb," Tree replied.

"But determined to bring Kelly's killer to justice," Freddie added.

Tree looked at her. "Yes, something like that, I suppose, although with me out there trying to prove his innocence, Rex may well conclude his goose is cooked."

"You knew Kelly better than anyone here. So right at this moment, I would have to say you are Rex's best bet—maybe his only bet."

Tree was silent. Freddie added, "Not to put any pressure on you."

"I'm not certain I ever knew Kelly—or any of my ex-wives for that matter."

"Maybe you didn't want to know them," Freddie said.

"With Kelly, there was always what she said, and then what she said she was thinking, and then what she was really thinking, and often enough all those things were very different." Tree glanced at his wife. "You had lunch with her recently. How did she seem?"

"As I told you, not all that happy. Nothing you could put your finger on, just this sense that she wasn't exactly ecstatic about being on the island."

Tree hesitated before he finally said, "Unless."

"Unless what?"

"It was Rex."

"Or you," Freddie said pointedly.

"There you go," Tree said.

"For what it's worth, I don't think either one of you killed her," Freddie said.

"Then who?"

"That's what we're paying you the big bucks to find out," Freddie said

"Then I'd better get to work."

"I want you to drop me off at the store," Freddie said. "I'm late for a meeting."

"Is everything all right?"

Now it was her turn to hesitate. "I'm not sure," she said. "I think that's the most truthful way to put it."

"Sorry," he said. "You mentioned something the other night about a fight at work, and then with Rex's arrest and everything, I forgot all about it."

"Understandable," Freddie said. "But now I have to deal with it this morning."

"Deal with what?"

"It's complicated," Freddie answered with a sigh, "but as I told you before, I have investors who are spending a lot of time studying the bottom line. They don't particularly like what they are seeing."

"Which means?"

"It could mean they want me out—or some of them want me out."

"Out of Dayton's?"

"Out of the business, yes," Freddie said.

"Who wants this?"

"Certain members of the board."

"You're kidding. You're the one who brought these guys in originally."

"Welcome to my corporate world."

"I don't believe this," Tree said.

"It took me by surprise, too," Freddie said. "But they are not happy with what they are getting from the stores."

"But the stores are doing well, aren't they?"

"They are not doing well enough in the estimation of some board members. They had certain expectations that have yet to be achieved. They believe I am responsible for the shortfall. Therefore, like I say, some members of the board want to replace me."

"Can they do that?"

"We will see," Freddie said.

8

After dropping Freddie off at Dayton's, Tree drove up to Captiva Island and parked in the drive at Andy Rosse Lane. He couldn't face going inside the house. Going into the house would mean he had to come up with some idea of how to go about investigating his ex-wife's murder. He had no ideas; his mind was blank. Rex, Freddie, T. Emmett Hawkins—they were all expecting him to do something.

Except, he didn't know what to do.

He walked down Andy Rosse to the beach trying not to think about Rex, but concentrating instead on Freddie facing the prospect of losing everything she had worked so hard to achieve these past few years while he had floundered around like an idiot—the fool and his Sanibel Sunset Detective Agency.

Maybe if she hadn't been so distracted by his various misadventures, she wouldn't be in the trouble she apparently now found herself in with her board of directors.

And, as usual, he was helpless to do anything other than wring his hands and feel sorry for himself.

It was another deceptively sunny day on Captiva, the sort of day that could convince you everything was all right with the world when demonstrably it wasn't. Florida was not designed for unhappiness, but there he stood, unhappily—the darkness in a sunny place.

Tree took off his shoes, rolled his pants up around his ankles, and walked down to the water's edge. He allowed the surf to wash over his bare feet for a few minutes before beginning to stroll along the shore, sinking his bare feet into the wet sand, feeling the late morning sun beating on him. He wasn't going to be able to take this much exposure for long. He thought about the times he walked Clinton along the beach, the floppy-eared French hound who had so endeared himself to Freddie and him.

The next thing, he was choking with emotion, standing in the surf, gulping for air, overwhelmed by thoughts of love and loss, loss and love, the two going so well together as he marched through life toward the abyss, marrying everyone along the way.

What was wrong with him? He had asked himself that question lots of times over the years without getting any satisfactory answer. Rex had been his guiding light through the complicated maze of his stupidity for as long as he could remember, the calming voice in the night that got him through three marriages, not to mention the misfired relationships in between those marriages, their only saving grace being that they didn't end with him at an altar—often thanks to Rex's intervening wisdom.

Now his best friend, confidant, mentor, supporter and most trusted advisor was in jail, accused of murdering Tree's former wife, a woman Rex had always loved from afar and wanted for himself, even as he introduced her to Tree and then proceeded to act as best man at their wedding.

All these years later, Rex was poised to marry—who? The woman of his dreams?—except at the last moment, his long-held secret ambition finally within reach, that dream had shattered. Kelly walked away from the altar.

"Didn't you ever try something just because you were intrigued, only to find out it wasn't for you? Then you pay a big price for your little experiment, and it hangs over you and refuses to go away."

Kelly's last words to him. Did Rex briefly intrigue her, and that's as far as it went? Was that why she couldn't go through with the marriage? Rex in the end was a fling, no more than that. As he stood there, foamy surf washing over his feet, an image of a prospective killer formed in his mind: a man angry at being just a fling and rejected so publicly. Someone who in a fury might act in a way that led to something that never otherwise would have been contemplated.

The face formed in his mind. It looked a lot like Rex Baxter.

Tree's cellphone vibrated in his pocket. He wasn't going to answer it—he didn't want to talk to anyone right now—but then he thought better of it and pulled out the phone and swiped it open.

"Hello, Tree," a rather formal voice said. "This is Judy Markov."

For a moment, the name didn't register. "Yes?"

"It's Judy, Tree," the voice said. "Your ex-wife. Remember me?"

"Yes, sorry, of course. Judy. I'm in a fog here. Your married name threw me."

"I need to see you, Tree," she said.

"Are you sure that's a very good idea? Your husband wasn't exactly happy when he met me."

"Please, Tree. It is very important."

He gripped his phone tighter. "All right. When would you like to do this?"

"As soon as possible," she said.

Herds of tourists filled Andy Rosse Lane as Tree made his way back toward the house, the traffic along the street impossible. Even so, Tree could hardly miss the young man ambling toward him, the expectant smile glued to his face. Tree groaned. Not this again.

"Hey there, Mr. Callister. Long time no see."

Tommy Dobbs had put on weight since he left Sanibel and went to work for the *Chicago Sun-Times*, no longer so Ichabod Crane-thin. The acne that once tracked across his pasty face was gone too. And he dressed much better, a crisp, short-sleeved dress shirt, neatly creased linen slacks, a good pair of Bass shoes. Yet he retained the Ray-Ban sunglasses he wore the first time Tree met him when he was starting out as a private detective and Tommy was a rookie newsman at the *Island Reporter*.

"Tommy," Tree said, trying to sound enthusiastic.

Tommy frowned. "It's Thomas now, Mr. Callister. Thomas Dobbs."

"Sorry, uh, Thomas, I keep forgetting. How are you?"

"Thanks to you, Mr. Callister, never better. They love my stuff at the *Sun-Times*, and of course I always give you credit for turning my professional life around."

"And I'm always delighted to hear you're doing well in Chicago. What brings you back here? Vacation?"

"You always say that, Mr. Callister. You always think I'm here on vacation."

"I'm always hoping that's the case, Tommy."

Tommy blessed the observation with a sly smile, the kind of smile that could only be provided by a reporter who had been around the block a couple of times. Had Tommy been around the block? Not nearly enough, Tree surmised. He could easily resent that smile.

"Come on, Mr. Callister, I think you know as well as I do why I'm here."

"I'm afraid I don't know a thing," Tree said. He started walking again.

Tommy caught up with him and fell into step. "Rex Baxter, Mr. Callister, former Hollywood actor, popular WBBM-TV weatherman for many years. Accused of murdering his fiancée Kelly Fleming, once the number-one news anchor in Chicago—and the ex-wife of legendary reporter and ace private detective, Tree Callister."

"I'm retired—from newspapers and private detecting."

"I'm sorry for what's happened to your ex-wife and your best pal, Mr. Callister, I truly am. But you've got to admit this is one heck of a story—and my editors have sent me back here to get it."

"Good for you, Tommy, or Thomas, but you're not going to get it from me."

"Mr. Callister, you always tell me that."

"I always tell you a lot of things, Tommy. Trouble is you don't seem to listen to any of them."

"At least give me a statement, for old time's sake."

"That's what you always say."

"That's because sometimes it works," Tommy said, once again delivering that sly smile. "So please, let me have a quote."

"No."

The sly smile disappeared, replaced by the hang-dog expression Tommy was able to produce on the occasions when he wanted something Tree wasn't willing to give him. "I'm under the gun, Mr. Callister. I've got to file something for the website in the next twenty minutes or so, and they also want a video feed for later. Please, help me out here. They think I've got sort of an in with you."

Tree came to a stop and turned to face Tommy. Beneath the Ray-Bans his eager face shone in the sunlight. Tree sighed. "All right, here's a quote you can use: Rex Baxter is an innocent man. He would never harm anyone, let alone the woman he loved."

As Tree spoke, Tommy waved a pocket voice recorder under his nose. He said, "If Rex Baxter didn't kill Kelly Fleming, Mr. Callister, will you be tracking down her killer, bringing him to justice?"

"That's it, Tommy," Tree said. "I have nothing more to say."

Tree walked on, Tommy hurrying to catch up with him. "If you need my help cracking this case, Mr. Callister..."

"I'm not cracking any case."

"If you need my help, let me know. I'm there for you. I really like Rex, and I want to help in any way I can."

"You can help me by staying out of my hair," Tree said.

"You say that right now, Mr. Callister," Tommy called as Tree ducked into his house. "But don't underestimate me."

"I never underestimate you, Tommy."

"And I'll bet you can use my help!"

9

Bailey Road curved off Periwinkle Way and in the process changed its name to Bay Shore Drive. A parking area at the bend in the road fronted a strip of beach with a view of the causeway linking Sanibel Island to the mainland. Judy, his ex-wife, was waiting when he got there, sitting inside a gray Jaguar. His first wife in a Jaguar, that was something to see, Tree thought. The new Judy. The rich Judy. The Judy he would never have expected in a million years.

She got out of the car as he parked. The day had become overcast. The causeway was a thin line in the mist shrouding the bay. He thought as he came to a stop a few paces in front of her that she was still a handsome woman, despite the weight that the years had added.

"Thanks for coming, Tree," she said with a winsome smile. "I know this is not a good time."

"It's all right. I've felt bad ever since the Lighthouse. That whole thing was…awkward."

"Terribly," she agreed.

"I'm glad we have a chance to talk."

"I'm so sorry to hear about Rex," she said.

"It's a bad situation," Tree said. Well, that was understating it, he thought.

"I hadn't realized he was involved with Kelly."

"He was about to marry her."

"The woman you left me for."

"That's not true. I know what you think, but it's not true."

The winsome smile disappeared. Her eyes flickered away from him. "You really were an awful husband," she said.

"Guilty as charged," Tree said.

"Of course, you wouldn't admit to a thing in those days," she said.

"I've had some time to think about it," Tree said. "I could have done a lot better."

"I'm not even sure why you married me. You really had no interest in marriage."

"Judy, it was so long ago," was all he could think of to say.

"Yes, I was three wives ago, wasn't I? I'm surprised you even remember me."

"Judy, we had two children together; I remember."

"Our troubled Chris," she said. "Troubled, difficult Chris."

"He's doing better now," Tree said.

"Yes, I suppose he is. I think he wishes you would spend more time with him."

"My failings are many." Tree once again grappling for some sort of response that didn't sound totally lame.

Failing.

She said, "Chris thought I was insane to marry Alexei."

"Were you?"

"I don't know, I suppose I was," she said, distractedly. She rubbed at her forearms as if suddenly cold and walked a few paces away, the distance perhaps making conversation easier.

"He came to Chicago on some business thing or another. Do you remember Denver Jordan?"

"The Chicago developer. Sable Development. Chris told me you had gone to work for him."

"I was his executive assistant. He introduced me to Alexei a couple of years ago. It was quite a whirlwind affair. He flew me to Moscow. This fabulous home he has in the suburbs, a palace, really. And the next thing I knew, I was agreeing to marry him."

"Too much vodka," Tree said.

She looked at him ruefully. "Or not enough."

Judy ceased rubbing at her arms and came back to where Tree was standing. "I don't know anyone here—except you."

"But you'll meet other people. It's a friendly island."

"That's not what I mean."

"What do you mean, Judy?"

"It means I am frightened and have nowhere to turn."

"You're frightened of Alexei?"

"I probably shouldn't be telling you any of this."

"No, it's all right," Tree said.

"He hasn't done anything, not really. It's just that..." She stopped and began rubbing at her arms again.

"It's what?"

"The other day the insurance company sent a letter. I usually open the mail that comes to our home. I didn't even think about it, I just opened it. It was a form letter, confirming that Alexei had changed the beneficiary of his life insurance."

"To you?"

"That's the thing. I am no longer the beneficiary."

"Who is?"

"A woman named Elin Danielsen."

"His mistress."

The winsome smile was back, slightly more knowing this time. "You've done your homework."

"I couldn't resist knowing more about the man my former wife married."

"He doesn't make much effort to hide his involvement with her."

"How do you feel about that?"

"He says it comes with the territory. All Russian men of what he calls his stature have mistresses. It's something I must understand."

"And do you?"

"I guess I do—or at least I tolerate it."

"So if he dies, she gets his life insurance, not you. Why is that so scary? I assume that as his wife, you're taken care of."

"I'm not so sure," she said. "The people who displease Alexei have a way of disappearing."

"Does that include wives?"

"His first wife was lost on a Mediterranean cruise. They said it was an accident. A girlfriend was found dead in her apartment. That was supposedly a suicide. The authorities questioned Alexei in both instances, but nothing ever happened."

"Did you know any of this when you married him?"

Judy shook her head. "I was a naïve woman at a time in my life when I could only be thrilled that a man of Alexei's wealth appeared interested. I didn't find out about the mistresses—or the disappearances—until was too late."

"So you're afraid you may be the next wife to disappear."

"These oligarchs—and Alexei is certainly one of them—they live by their own rules. If they don't like something, they order it changed. If they are tired of someone, that person goes away, and in today's Russia no questions are asked."

"But this is America and you're an American citizen, and no one thinks a whole lot of rich Russians these days."

"That's all true, except Alexei this morning announced we are returning to Moscow."

"This after you discover you're no longer the beneficiary of his life insurance."

"Do you wonder why I'm nervous?"

"When does he want to leave?"

"He says he's not sure, but soon. That scares me, too. The not knowing."

"Don't go with him."

"Alexei can be very persuasive. What's more, he is surrounded by people who will do what he orders them to do. If he wants me in Moscow, then there is a great likelihood I will be in Moscow, and if that happens, all bets are off."

"What about the police?" The Freddie Stayner answer to every crisis.

She grimaced. "What can the police do? He hasn't done anything. He hasn't even really said anything."

"Then what can I do to help?"

She stepped closer and embraced him. For a wild moment, he thought she was going to kiss him. Instead, she moved abruptly back. "Stay here a moment," she said.

She went over to where she had parked the Jaguar. She came back a few moments later with a thick sealed manila envelope. "Keep this in a safe place," she said, pressing the envelope into his hands.

"What is it?" he asked.

"It's the way you can be my friend, Tree. The way you can make up for so much of what happened in the past. The way you can help. I would beg you not to look inside. Not right now. It's better if you don't, and please don't talk to anyone about this. Not even Freddie. Can you do that for me?"

"If that's what you want, yes."

"It's better this way, believe me," Judy said. "Just hang onto it for now. I'll be in touch."

The smile wasn't at all winsome this time, Tree thought. This time it had a hard brittle quality about it. You could read a lot of things into that smile, things Tree had never thought to read when they were married.

"Let me know when you want it back," he said.

She looked relieved. "Thank you. You may be saving my life."

He was about to suggest she was being melodramatic. Then he saw the look on her face and decided to keep quiet. She kissed his cheek and went back to the Jaguar.

He held the manila envelope in his hands. The mist all but obscured the causeway.

10

Tree was surprised to see Freddie's Mercedes in the drive when he got back to Andy Rosse Lane. Too early for her to be home. Far too early.

He found her down on the terrace. She had changed out of business professional into her away-from-work uniform, shorts and a white T-shirt. She was sipping on a glass of sparkling water. When she saw him, she rose from the chair and intercepted him, her arms snaking around his neck, drawing him to her, burying her face in his shoulder.

And that's when he knew.

"It can't have happened this fast," he said.

"It did and it didn't," she said, her voice muffled against him. "But it happened, and that's it."

"There must be something you can do," he said.

"There is, I suppose, but I'm not sure I'm going to do it."

She held him tighter a moment longer and then broke away. There were no tears. When he lost his job at the *Sun-Times*, he was a blubbering basket case. With Freddie, there would be no emotional displays. She was tough; she would absorb the blows and move on.

"I'm tired of it all," she said, "the grind every day, the continuous reinvention of wheels that shouldn't have to be reinvented. I came here because the business in Chicago had worn me down, only to get worn down by the business here."

"But you love it," Tree said.

"Love it. Hate it. I don't know. Whatever, it's time for a change, something different."

"I feel like I'm responsible for this," Tree said.

"Don't. It's business and these things happen in business."

"Yeah, but how many executives are distracted by husbands getting themselves shot from time to time?"

"There is that," Freddie agreed. She slipped into his arms again. "But then not many executives have a husband like you."

"That statement could be read a number of different ways."

"It's a compliment, you dope." She kissed him. "Look at the number of women you've persuaded to marry you. That says something right there, doesn't it?"

"Not much that's good." They both laughed and he held her close.

"Can I get you a glass of wine?"

She grinned and said, "Sure, why not celebrate the end of something, the beginning of something else."

"The question is, what?"

She said in a teasing voice, "Maybe I'll become a detective on Sanibel Island."

That was his cue to go inside and pour her a glass of chardonnay. When he returned and handed her the glass, she asked him where he had been and he told her about his encounter with Judy, leaving out the part about the envelope. "She wanted to make amends for that meeting at the Lighthouse," Tree said.

"Where her Russian oligarch husband threatened you," Freddie said.

"I think she's a little afraid of him," Tree said.

"The women in your life are making things very complicated for you," Freddie continued. "Your first wife is frightened of her husband. Your second wife has been indicted on fraud charges. Your third wife has been murdered, and your best friend charged with the crime. And now your fourth wife has just become unemployed."

He kissed her. "Under the circumstances there is only one thing a detective can do."

"What's that?" She kissed him back.

"What the tough, two-fisted detective always does on these occasions. He takes the beautiful blonde into his bedroom."

"Good idea," Freddie said. "Except for one thing."

"What's that?"

"I'm doing the taking."

And she did.

———————

Tree sat up, trying to focus, wondering what time it was. He was in a bed—the ornate brass frame was lovely—but it wasn't his own. Through the brasswork he could see an oval mirror, a woman on a wicker seat in front of it, her skirt hiked to her hips, attaching a silk stocking to a garter. The woman, a violet-eyed, raven-haired beauty, looked up, and when she saw Tree, she smiled provocatively.

"I thought you'd never wake up," she said.

"Where am I?" Tree said, trying to shake himself fully awake.

"You're in my bedroom, where most men eventually find themselves." She stood up, smoothing her skirt, showing off a spectacular figure housed in the skirt and a white blouse that failed to hide her blazing sexuality.

"I shouldn't be here," Tree said.

The woman smiled knowingly. "Everyone says that. You shouldn't be here, but here you are."

"When I saw you as a kid, all those movies and the magazine stories about you breaking up marriages, my hormones went crazy."

"In those days," she said, "I was, well, I was like a cat on a hot tin roof."

"I probably couldn't have gotten through adolescence without you."

"You've been in my bedroom for a long time," she said.

"But not anymore," Tree said. "I'm grown up. I don't need the fantasy of you any longer."

"We can debate whether men ever grow up, especially where sex is concerned," she said. "But putting that aside, you probably need me more than ever."

"You think so?"

She nodded. "Let's face it, when you think in terms of too many marriages and too many divorces, you probably think of me."

"Yes, I suppose I do," Tree admitted. "How many times did you marry? Was it six?"

"Eight, actually," she said.

"I'm embarrassed to have done it four times; it's something I think about a lot. How did you get through eight?"

She smiled again and said, "You take them one at a time, baby, and you believe. Every time you believe this is the right one. It's a job for an optimist, that's for certain."

"Or a fool," Tree said.

"Not a fool," she replied. "Just foolish. There's a difference."

"Yes, I suppose there is. What I can't figure out is how it happened. How I ended up being married four times."

She drifted back to seat herself, once again facing the oval mirror. When she spoke, she addressed the image in the mirror as much as Tree. "You want to know what my problem was, honestly? I could never find a man who could handle me. I was too much for all my husbands. They weren't tough enough."

"What about Richard Burton?"

"I loved Richard more than the others. But even he couldn't keep up." As she spoke she cocked her head to one side and patted at her hair. "He kept having these guilt feelings about who he was and how we lived and what we were doing. I took it all in stride. A vodka and orange juice first thing in the morning helped. But Richard had to drink himself under a table to get through it."

She stopped adjusting hair that needed no adjusting, turning away from the mirror so that she could face Tree. "Baby, there are no answers in marriage, only more questions and eventual failure. No matter what you think or how much you hope, you end up alone, maybe with a few good memories, but I even wonder about the memories. I mean, what's to remember about Nicky Hilton?"

"No," Tree protested. "There is more to it than that. I've found happiness. I have. It took a while, but I finally met the right person."

"It's all wrapped in deceit and duplicity," she said, rising from the dressing table bench and coming toward him. "Whatever the truth today, baby, it will turn out to be the lie tomorrow."

She sank onto the bed, the full sensuality of her closing in, the power of the universal sex symbol unleashed. "Just forget everything for now, baby. Come back to the fantasy that's always sustained you. Lose yourself in it. That's where it's the purest and most honest. Come on, don't just lie there. What are you waiting for? This is what you've always wanted..."

"No..."

"Come to me...Come..."

"Tree," a voice called. "Tree."

He struggled awake. A vision loomed over him and after a moment formed itself into something recognizable: Freddie, concern shadowing her face. "Wake up," she said. "You were dreaming again."

"Yes," he said.

"Better get dressed," Freddie said. "Rex's arraignment is this morning."

11

Rex Baxter, drawn and pale, appeared in the prisoners' box at the Lee County Courthouse in an orange jumpsuit. The jumpsuit shocked Tree. Chicago's most beloved TV weatherman, the prince of Sanibel and Captiva islands, the matchless raconteur who had slept with Joan Crawford, drank in Rome with Sinatra and Hemingway, acted in a movie with Elvis Presley, the guy who had been with him through thick and thin over the years—in an orange jumpsuit! Freddie, seated beside Tree in the visitors' gallery, having much the same reaction, held her husband's hand tight.

Tree had encountered the assistant district attorney, Lee Bixby previously, and he didn't like him. Bixby was a short, aggressive young prosecutor with dark, thinning hair, close-cropped to add to his air of a malevolent crow. He argued that given the severity of the charges against Rex, the president of the Sanibel-Captiva Chamber of Commerce should not be granted bail.

T. Emmett Hawkins, resplendent in a beige linen suit that even at eleven o'clock in the morning remained wrinkle free, countered with the usual arguments: Rex was a long-time Sanibel resident, a community leader with the highest reputation, a man of a certain age, a highly unlikely flight risk and certainly no danger to the community.

The arguments fell on the deaf ears of Judge J. Ethel Rispoli, who had a reputation almost as hard-nosed as Bixby's, and who dispensed justice with the emotionless efficiency of someone working an assembly line. Bail was summarily denied. Rex would remain in custody. As they led him away, Rex briefly caught Tree's eye. The ghost of a smile, disconcerting for a man not known for his ghostly smiles. Tree felt worse than ever.

"I'm not surprised," Hawkins said outside the courtroom, "given the nature of the charges."

"Still, it's a disappointment," Freddie said.

"I'm meeting with our friend Lee Bixby this afternoon so I should have a better idea of what exactly the prosecution has. I'm sure he's going to offer some sort of plea deal."

"But you're not going to take it, are you?"

Instead of answering immediately in the negative, Hawkins moved his shoulders up and down in an elaborate shrug. "Let's see what they have to say."

"Rex is innocent." Freddie said this with a believer's flat certainty.

Hawkins turned to Tree. "How are you coming with your investigation?"

"So far, I don't have much to report." The words sounded lame, even to him.

"Keep on it," Hawkins admonished. "As I stated earlier, if Rex is not the killer, then someone is. Find that person. Meanwhile, I'll find out what Bixby has to say, talk to Rex, and get back to you."

After Hawkins left, Freddie said to Tree, "So what are you going to do?"

Tree just looked at her, at a loss for words. "You've got to do something," Freddie said. "You are the Sanibel Sunset Detective, after all."

"Not anymore," Tree said.

"Maybe it's time you went back to work," Freddie said.

"I never thought I'd hear you say that," Tree said.

"I never thought we'd be standing here wondering how to get Rex out of jail."

Tree spotted Tommy Dobbs coming down the hall. He excused himself from Freddie and went to meet Tommy. The reporter's face lit up when he saw Tree.

"Mr. Callister," he beamed. "I was just coming to get a quote from you."

"Never mind the quote. Are you serious about helping me?"

Tommy nodded. "Sure I am. What can I do?"

"Get on the phone to any contacts you might have in Chicago. Rex didn't kill Kelly Fleming, but someone did. Maybe there's someone in her past: a boyfriend we don't know about, someone who might be angry enough to hurt her."

"Any ideas who that might be?"

Tree shook his head. "Until Kelly showed up on Sanibel with Rex, I hadn't heard from her in years. I have no idea what she was up to in Chicago. That's what I want you to find out. Do you think you can do that for me?"

"I can sure give it a try, Mr. Callister."

"As soon as you find something, get back to me. We don't have a whole lot of time."

"I'll get on it right away." He paused and then said, "There is something else."

"What's that?"

"There is a lot of speculation floating around. Many people don't believe Rex was capable of murder. They're talking about other possible suspects."

"Who are they talking about?"

"They are talking about you, Mr. Callister."

"People think I killed Kelly?"

"Did you, Mr. Callister?"

Tree gave Tommy a look. "Get on the phone to Chicago, Tommy."

"Thomas, Mr. Callister. Like I keep telling you, it's Thomas."

12

Inmates at the Lee County Jail were allowed two visitors per week, although "visit" was something of a misnomer. One could not actually sit with an inmate; in this high-tech age a "visit" amounted to viewing the inmate on a video monitor; a form of Skyping, Tree supposed.

Accordingly, Tree and Rex "Skyped" for the first time in their long lives once Tree had been added to the Inmate's Authorized Visitation List, and appeared at the Visitation Center on Ortiz Avenue. He showed his identification, and was frisked for possible contraband before being seated in front of a flat screen bolted to the wall.

"You're back on television," Tree said when Rex's image flickered on the monitor in front of him.

"Where I belong," Rex said with a thin smile. "Tomorrow's weather is cloudy with very little chance of relief."

"I think you're being too pessimistic about the forecast," Tree said.

"I hope so," Rex said. "But I discovered when I was a weatherman, you never go wrong with a little pessimism."

"If I remember correctly, your forecasts were seldom very accurate."

"Nobody was more effective at screwing up the weather," Rex agreed.

"I hate to ask something clichéd like, 'How are you doing?' But how are you doing?"

"Funny thing," Rex said, "for years I've been trying to keep you out of jail. Now here I am in jail."

"How are they treating you? Any trouble?"

"No trouble," Rex said. "I'm too old to bother with much. Most of the convicts are young guys, and they're okay, except when I tell them about Joan Crawford or Hemingway, they don't have a clue who I'm talking about."

"I'm going to get you out of here," Tree said.

Rex said, "Yeah? Did you bring a hacksaw?"

"I'm going to find Kelly's killer," Tree said.

"Oh, goodie," Rex said.

"You don't sound very reassured."

"No offense Tree, but with you out there tracking down the killer, I'm liable to rot in here for the rest of my life."

"You should be more of an optimist," Tree said.

"My experience, as I mentioned, causes me to lean toward pessimism," Rex said.

"Any ideas who might have wanted Kelly dead?"

"No," Rex said.

"She didn't talk about her past, someone she might have broken up with before she met you, a jealous lover?"

"She never spoke about who she had been involved with before I came along—except you, of course."

"How was she acting this past couple of weeks? Did you notice anything different about her?"

Rex thought for a moment. "I suppose in retrospect she was a bit moody. She seemed irritated at times, and then she would snap out of it, and we'd have a great time together, and I would reassure myself that everything was okay and we were going to make it together."

"Any idea what was making her moody?"

"Again, in retrospect, you'd have to say it was me—or the prospect of marrying me. I'd be a fool to believe otherwise, considering she walked away from the altar about five minutes before we were supposed to be married."

"After she walked out, did you talk to her?"

"I tried to, but she said there was nothing to talk about. She said she didn't want to hurt me any more than she already had. She said she was going back to Chicago."

"Was she still at your place?"

"No, she was staying at the Holiday Inn on the island. She came around to pick up her things."

"Did you talk?"

"Again, I tried. But she said there was nothing to talk about. Her mind was made up."

"So she wasn't staying with you?"

"No. I told you, the Holiday Inn."

"But you were there when she came around to pick up her things."

"That's right. When she said there was nothing to talk about, that she had no choice, I left."

"Why did you leave?"

"I was upset. Angry. I didn't want to be there with her. I thought it best if I just got out."

"And when you left, she was all right?"

"Yes. She was fine, aside from her finger. She cut her finger."

"She said she had 'no choice'? What did she mean by that?"

"She had a choice. She could have married me."

"But maybe there was something else, something that made her decide not to go through with the wedding."

"You talked to her. What do you think? Was she trying to hide something?"

"All she said to me was that she couldn't go through with it. Not much more than that. After you left the house, where did you go?"

"I went to my office."

"Did anyone see you?"

"Sure. Lots of people. I didn't feel a whole lot like talking to anyone. I sat there for a while and then went over to your place and fell asleep on your sofa."

"When the police arrived, that was the first time you knew what had happened to Kelly?"

"Yes, of course it was," Rex said.

"And the police had been called by your pool guy."

"It's a woman, actually. But, yeah, that's what they told me."

"Not much to go on," Tree said.

"You don't have anything to go on," Rex replied. "Listen to me, Tree. You're better off staying out of this. I'm in enough trouble. I don't need you getting into trouble, too."

"I won't get into trouble."

"You always say that—just before you get yourself into a load of trouble."

"Don't worry about me," Tree said.

"I am worried about you. Just remember, I'm not going to be there to bail you out when you get yourself up a certain creek without a paddle."

"I love you," Tree said.

"What's that? Code for 'I haven't heard a word you've said?'"

"Not at all," Tree grinned. "It simply means I love you."

"Yeah, well, I love you, too. But this time, do me a big favor and listen to me. Stay out of it—and come back and see me in a week or so. It's kind of lonely in here."

"By then, I'll have you out," Tree said.

On the television monitor Rex made a show of rolling his eyes.

13

A blue Chevrolet Spark with a big dent in its side was parked in the drive when Tree got back to Andy Rosse Lane. He thought a tourist had left it there and he was fuming as he entered the house. He stopped when he heard the sound of someone sobbing. What fresh hell was this? He silently thanked Dorothy Parker for providing him with the catch phrase for his life.

The sound was coming through the open glass doors leading down to the terrace. That's where he found his fourth wife consoling his third, Patricia Laine.

"Skye," Freddie amended. "Pat wants to be called Skye now."

Pat, or Skye, raised a tear-stained face and said, "Hello, Tree. I really appreciate this."

He groaned inwardly. Dorothy Parker had it comparatively easy. She had only liquor and her own genius with which to deal. He had wives—and no genius in sight.

"You really appreciate what?" Tree said.

"Skye's in trouble," Freddie said, as if that was something he should know. "She's going to stay with us for a while until things cool off a bit."

"Until what cools off?"

Pat's hand was on Freddie's arm. "This is so kind of you," she said and then began sobbing some more.

Freddie put her arm around Pat. "It's all right, Skye. You can stay as long as you like."

Tree stood gaping at the two women seated together, words failing him. "Can someone answer me? What's got to cool off?"

Freddie gave him a slightly irritated look, as though he should know very well what had to cool off. "Skye's boyfriend has been threatening her."

"I'm so scared," Pat added, as if to clinch the news that she was being threatened.

"What boyfriend?" Tree demanded.

"Tal," Pat burbled.

"Tal? You mean your lawyer, Tal Fiala?"

Pat managed a nod.

"The guy who's been indicted with you for defrauding the elderly lady?"

"I'm innocent," Pat said.

"The widow suffering from Alzheimer's," Tree went on.

"They're not actually sure it's Alzheimer's," Pat said. "It could be another form of dementia."

"I didn't know that," Tree said sarcastically. "That puts a whole different spin on things."

"Tree, that's enough," Freddie said in a warning voice. "Skye's been through a lot. Tal showed up at her door last night, drunk, and waving a gun around, threatening to kill her."

"Did you call the police?" Tree said.

Pat managed a shake of her head. "The Palm Beach police are on Tal's side. He's rich. He pays them off. They hate me. They're out to get me."

"She got in her car and drove over here," Freddie said, as though that explained everything.

"I didn't know where else to go." Pat resumed her sobbing.

Freddie's consoling embrace went back to work. "It's all right, Skye. You're safe now."

Tree wondered about that, but knew better than to say anything.

Freddie settled Pat in the guest bedroom, where she could get some sleep. "She's dead tired poor thing," Freddie said when she returned to the terrace.

"Just to remind you, she's under indictment in Palm Beach for defrauding an elderly demented woman out of millions of dollars."

"Skye says it was Tal Fiala who took the money. She had no idea what he was doing. She was a woman blinded by love."

"Forgive my callousness, but I find it hard to think of Pat as a woman blinded by much, least of all love," Tree said.

"Let's face it, Tree. You are somewhat prejudiced, aren't you?"

"Where Pat is concerned, I'm afraid I am."

"She wants to be called Skye now," Freddie said.

"This week," Tree said. "With Pat, next week it could easily be something else."

"And I think you should be a little more sympathetic. She's obviously troubled, and she may well be in danger. This is domestic violence, Tree, and I don't like it when you don't take it seriously."

"I take it seriously," Tree protested.

"We have an obligation to protect her."

"You are amazing," Tree said. "How many other women would welcome their husband's ex-wife into their home?"

"It's the least we can do for her," Freddie said. "And speaking of wives…"

"I seem to speak of nothing else these days."

"You went to see Rex this morning. How's he doing?"

"He's not an ex-wife," Tree said.

"He was about to marry one of yours. Besides, the two of you have been practically married for years."

"I'm too tired to argue the point—and you may be right."

"So how's he holding up?"

"All right under the circumstances, I suppose. You know Rex. He never gives away too much. He says he doesn't want me involved in this."

"That's curious. Why not?"

"I believe he's worried that with me poking around, he's certain to end up in jail for the rest of his life."

They both laughed halfheartedly, and then Freddie said, "But seriously, does he have any idea who might have killed Kelly?"

Tree shook his head. "He says she was a bit moody leading up to the wedding. But the first real indication he had that something was wrong was when she walked out of the ceremony."

"Yes, that was certainly an indication," Freddie said.

"I've asked Tommy Dobbs to look into Kelly's life in Chicago, to see if she was involved with someone who might have wanted to hurt her."

"And she said nothing to you—when you followed her out to the parking lot that morning?"

"She said that sometimes you try something because it intrigues you, but then you discover it's not for you, but you have to live with it."

"That's strange, don't you think?"

"I thought she was talking about Rex," Tree said.

"Or maybe it was you."

"I'm not sure what to think—or what to do next," Tree said.

"On television, the detective always visits the crime scene and comes up with something the police missed."

"Yes, well, good luck with that," Tree said.

"Have you been over to Rex's house?"

"Not lately," Tree said.

"It might be worth a visit," Freddie said. "You never know."

14

Rex's house set back from the road among tall palms, was now decorated with lines of yellow crime scene tape, transforming what had been a pleasant bungalow on a quiet Sanibel Island street into reality show notoriety. Even in bright afternoon sunshine the yellow tape lent an air of menace.

Tree's best friend lived here. His former wife had died here. This was not a place he was anxious to visit, but Freddie was right. He had to look around, although he had no illusions about finding evidence that the police hadn't.

Rolled copies of the *Fort Myers Times-Herald*, turning yellow, had been thrown up onto the front steps, the subscriber off to jail before he could cancel delivery. Tree made a mental note to do it for him.

He ducked under the tape, collected the papers, and went around to the rear of the house, deposited the papers into a plastic garbage bin, and then used the key Rex had given him a couple of years before to unlock the door and get inside.

Curtains were drawn across the big front windows in the living room, keeping the interior dim. An open box of muesli stood on the counter in the kitchen. A half pot of coffee remained in the coffee maker. Breakfast dishes were piled in the sink. It looked like someone had left unexpectedly but would soon be back. Well, Rex certainly left quickly. But how soon he would return was an open question.

He crossed to the windows and opened the curtains. Sunlight flooded the living room, illuminating dusty surfaces, white walls, and a framed poster for *G.I. Blues*, the Elvis Presley movie in which the young Rex had a small role back in the days when he was going to become a big Hollywood star.

What was he looking for? He wasn't sure. Proof that Rex was an innocent man? Yes, that was it. The private investigator investigating. Finding something the police had missed. Something that would immediately establish his best friend's innocence. That's what he was supposed to be doing, wasn't it? Fine, but the only evidence of anything was that other than the *G.I. Blues* poster, Rex didn't expose much of his personal life in the living room.

Back in the kitchen, Tree reviewed the evidence of Rex's seemingly hurried exit. Why did Rex have to leave so fast? If Kelly came around to pick up her things, then presumably there would be no hurry, and Rex being Rex and no slob, he would have had time to clean up before going to his office.

Or maybe he was so distraught by Kelly's presence, her unwillingness to talk about what had happened, that he had to get out of the house and away from her, and just left everything.

Yes, that could be it.

He entered the master bedroom. Photographs in silver frames topped the chest of drawers: Rex with Kelly at a long-ago WBBM party in Chicago; Rex with Kelly again, a more contemporary photo taken at the Lighthouse Restaurant; Tree and Rex, arms entwined, next to the *Former Actor II* the day he took delivery of the craft; Rex posing happily with Ronald Reagan, two former actors who made good, more or less.

The bed hadn't been made before Rex's departure. Rex's clothes hung neatly in a walk-in closet on one side, Kelly's clothes on the other. There were reminders of Kelly's presence not only in the bedroom—an intricate necklace atop the dresser adjacent to a pair of earrings—but in the bathroom, too: the lingering scent of her perfume; a hairbrush; a jar of Lancôme facial cream; Tom Ford Neroli Portofino body lotion; a shower cap.

But then if Kelly had come to the house to collect her belongings, why were clothes still hanging in the closet? None of her things in the bathroom looked as though they had been moved. Did her killer interrupt her before she was able to pack up anything?

Lingering here inhaling a dead woman's scent, lamenting the way life had unfolded, regretting the unfairness of it all, was not going to help anything. Neither were his doubts about Rex. He didn't do it; couldn't have done it.

He returned to the living room, and then went out to the pool with its flagstone deck, the pool house on the far side, a flowering garden surrounding the flagstones. These were the stones against which, according to the prosecution, Kelly's head was slammed, causing her death. There was no sign of that today.

Tree looked around him. In one corner a plastic sign was stretched between two metal wires shoved into the earth. The sign read: BRITTANY POOLS. Beneath it was a telephone number and a website, brittanypools.com.

Tree heard something behind him and turned in time to glimpse Owen Markfield an instant before the detective shoved the palm of his hand into Tree's chest and knocked him backwards.

"What the hell are you doing here?" Markfield demanded. A characteristic display of anger stained the perfection of his face—characteristic at least when he encountered Tree. He wore the loose-fitting Tommy Bahama blue-striped shirt and white slacks that made him appear less like a cop, more like the social director of a resort hotel irritated by one of the guests.

When Tree failed to answer his question immediately, Markfield gave him another shove. "Did you hear me? What are you doing here?"

"Hey, you're assaulting a citizen," Tree said, angrily.

"I'm pushing around a piece of shit," Markfield said. "Performing a public service. Now tell me what you're doing here."

"There were newspapers strewn all over the front steps," Tree said. "I thought I'd clean them up."

"This is still an active crime scene, you dummy. Out of bounds."

"I'm just trying to help my friend," Tree said.

That drew a smirk from Markfield. "You? You're trying to help? That's great news for the prosecution. With you on Baxter's side, he's sure to be convicted."

"Come on, Markfield, I know we've had our issues in the past, but don't take this out on Rex."

"Take it out on Rex?" Markfield looked genuinely surprised. "What do you think I am, anyway? Believe me, I would like nothing better than to nail your ass to the wall. But that has nothing to do with arresting Rex Baxter."

"I don't believe you really think he killed Kelly Fleming and then conveniently left her body in the pool house for someone to find."

"I don't know how convenient it was, but yeah, I believe he killed her in a fit of jealousy because she wouldn't marry him. All the evidence points to that—as you will soon see, Callister."

"And what evidence is that?"

The question brought out another smirk. "You know when we found the body, I put you down for the murder. Your ex-wife, marrying someone else, walking out."

"That's as crazy as thinking Rex did it," Tree said.

"Not so crazy. You're walking on the wild side. You know it, and I know it. And when you are playing that side of the street, I don't think there's anything you're not capable of, as you've demonstrated in the past. You killed once. Who's to say you wouldn't do it again?"

"Then why not arrest me?"

"Nothing would give me more pleasure, believe me," Markfield said. "Fortunately, for you, this time, your pal is the killer. But your turn is coming, Callister, don't worry. Now get out of here, before I arrest you for trespassing."

"You're making a big mistake," Tree said. "Rex didn't kill Kelly, but someone did, and he or she is still out there."

Markfield's face darkened. Fury lit his blue eyes. Only the spawn of the devil could possibly have eyes like that,

Tree thought. "Don't make me tell you again. Get the hell out of here."

Probably best to do as he was told, Tree decided.

15

Crossing the Cape Coral Bridge over the Caloosahatchee River, Tree turned north onto Del Prado Boulevard. A few blocks up, he found the headquarters for Brittany Pools in a mall with mission-style roof tiles.

Tree parked the Beetle beside a van with white paint peeling badly around its fenders. The Brittany Pools logo was shrink-wrapped on its sides. The logo featured a perky blond woman with a deep tan poured into a very small bikini. She smiled into the camera as she posed with a leaf skimmer beside a glistening in-ground swimming pool.

Inside the tiny shop, in front of a wallboard mounted with various pieces of cleaning apparatus, the same blond woman with the deep tan was behind the counter, without a leaf skimmer this time—or a bikini. Instead, she wore a white T-shirt and cut-off jean shorts. The smile she gave Tree was as perky as the one on the side of the truck. "Hi, there," she said brightly. "Are you enjoying your day so far?"

Given that a police officer had just told him his best friend was going to spend the rest of his life in prison and that he was intending to put Tree there, too, he was uncertain as to how enjoyable the day had been. He said something inane—"Thanks for asking"—and she blessed his response with another bright smile.

"You're Brittany?" he said.

"Brittany Pools. How may I be of service to you?"

Tree looked surprised. "Your name is actually Brittany Pools?"

"Neat, huh?" she said. "With a name like that, don't you know I just had to get into this business."

Tree fished his wallet out of his back pocket and showed her his State of Florida private investigator license, hoping she wouldn't notice that it had expired three months ago. Her eyes widened and the bright smile faded. He said, "I'm investigating the murder of Kelly Fleming."

Brittany's smile turned upside down. "I don't know," she said. "Am I supposed to be talking to you? I'm not sure the police want me talking to anyone about this."

"I'm a friend of Rex's," Tree said. "He's in jail, and I don't think he did this terrible thing, so I'm trying to help in any way I can."

"It was just so awful," she said in a rush of words signaling she wasn't too concerned about keeping quiet. "I went into the pool house to get some of the Pool Sparkle Purifier that I like to use. It gives the water a nice sheen, and it also reduces harmful UV rays, although, to be honest, I don't think Mr. Baxter ever used the pool enough to worry too much about UV rays."

"So you went into the pool house and found the body, is that it?"

She nodded solemnly. "I mean, like, I've never even seen a dead body before, except, I guess, on television. And I didn't really see her, if I'm being like totally honest."

"You didn't see Kelly?"

"I saw something, and that was enough for me. I closed the door and called the police."

"And the police identified the body?"

"Yes, I guess so. The first I heard was on the TV news later that night."

"What time was this?"

"You mean when I found the body?"

"That's right."

"The police asked me that, too. I guessed about two-thirty. The appointment was for two, and I'd been there for half an hour or so before I went looking for the Pool Sparkle."

"And no one was home?"

"I don't think I've ever actually seen Mr. Baxter at the house when I'm there. He's usually working—but that's not unusual. Very few of my clients are home when I clean their pools. I suppose that's why they need me to do it for them."

"Kelly Fleming was never there when you visited?"

"If she was, I never met her. She must have stayed in the house. I mean, a couple of times it seems to me there was a car in the driveway, but that was the only indication anyone was around."

Tree could not think of anything else to ask, and Brittany Pools did not have much else to say, except to keep repeating how awful it was. Tree gave Brittany his card and asked her to give him a call if she thought of anything else.

"That's what the police said, too."

"I'll bet they did," Tree said.

"I mean, for what it's worth..."

"Yes?" Tree said.

"I really like Mr. Baxter. Any time I saw him, he always told these great stories, even though I usually didn't know who he was talking about. I mean, he's a really nice guy."

"Yes, he is," Tree said.

"All I'm trying to say is that he really didn't strike me as the killer type."

"No," Tree said.

"Except that one time."

"One time?" Tree said.

"I got there and he was really yelling at someone. I mean screaming."

"You sure it was Rex?" Tree said.

"I thought it was. It sounded like him. Coming from inside the house. I couldn't make out what he was saying, but he was really, really angry. I had never heard him like that. I was kind of embarrassed, didn't want him to think I was, like, listening in on his conversation, so I left and did the next client, then came back a couple of hours later."

"Did you see him then?"

Brittany shook her head. "No, by that time he had left—at least it looked as though he had left."

"How long ago was this?"

"The last time I was there before I found the body. The week before."

"Did you tell the police this?"

She looked embarrassed. "I sort of had to, right?"

"Sure, of course. You had to be honest. Listen, thanks for your time."

"I'm sorry I can't be more helpful."

"You did fine, Brittany. I appreciate it."

"Tell Mr. Baxter I said hi, will you? I hope it works out for him."

Tree came out of Brittany's shop thinking about Rex's anger, reminded that he knew a side of Rex few people ever saw—a man who never lost his temper but when he did, it got truly lost. But that was a long time ago when they were both a lot younger and their fuses were a lot shorter. The angry side of Rex hadn't shown itself for many years. Rex talked about his Hollywood career with careless wit, everything turned into a good story. But Tree knew that his failure to do better in the movies had been a source of deep frustration that could boil over into white-hot anger.

But time and Sanibel Island had mellowed Rex. Or had it?

He got into the Beetle and sat there convincing himself that yes, time had calmed Rex. He was a much different person now. He was thinking this when he noticed a man get out of a Range Rover. The distinctive brush cut drew Tree's attention.

Alexei Markov's man, Valentin.

Entering Brittany Pools.

16

It was dusk before Valentin came out again. He paused to light a cigarette, and then walked to the Range Rover and got in. Tree debated whether to follow him, but as Valentin drove off, the cigarette dangling from the corner of his mouth, he decided to wait, curious what the Russian's visit might provoke from Brittany Pools.

An hour or so later when she did leave, Tree almost missed her. She went out the back and Tree had been watching the front and the van with the peeling white paint and the smiling Brittany on its sides.

He saw a red MGB pull around the corner of the building and come to stop at the edge of Del Prado Boulevard. Brittany's blond head shone in the fading daylight. As soon as there was a break in the traffic, she whipped the MGB onto the boulevard and headed south.

Tree kicked himself for his inattention, his lack of ability when it came to that most necessary of all tasks for any detective worth his salt, the stakeout. As he pushed the Beetle onto Del Prado, trying to spot the MGB, he concluded yet again that of all the second careers he might have pursued, private investigation should not even have been on the list.

Ahead, through the maze of evening traffic, he spotted the MGB and thanked the patron saints of detective work, whoever they were, that the car was painted red. He watched as it swung left onto the Cape Coral Bridge toward Fort Myers.

Brittany was a fast, impatient driver darting in and out of traffic so that Tree, in his rattling, aged Beetle, had trouble keeping up. Once on McGregor it became apparent she was headed for Sanibel Island. If that was the case, he was probably wasting his time—again. He should have followed Valentin instead. In all probability Brittany was up to nothing more duplicitous than cleaning a client's pool. But then if that was the case, why didn't she take her van? And what was Valentin doing at her office?

Once on the island, the traffic forced Brittany to slow down. The number of vehicles thinned on Sanibel-Captiva Road but Brittany kept to the speed limit, probably knowing the local cops liked to catch speeding young women in sports cars along this stretch. Just past the Castaways Beach and Cottages, at the moment Tree was certain she was going to cross Blind Pass onto Captiva, she made a right onto Mangrove Lane.

He managed to swerve off after her, a move so obvious that he was certain she would spot him. But by the time he finished thinking this, the tail end of the MGB was already disappearing onto Coconut Drive. He sped up, caution thrown away, as he came onto Coconut Drive. The MGB flashed in the waning light, perhaps two hundred yards ahead. It slowed and then turned left onto a palm-lined dirt roadway. As Tree drove past, he glimpsed electronic gates swinging open to admit the car.

By the time Tree parked the Beetle and hurried back to the entrance, the gates had closed, leaving him staring up at a high stone wall. Now what? Climb over the wall? He imagined security cameras following his every move. The police arriving shortly. The trespassing charge. The night in jail. The cross Freddie having to bail him out.

He had no choice but to get back into the Beetle and continue driving across Blind Pass onto Captiva Drive and home. He should do that. No question.

Then someone crashed into the gates.

Tree had turned away so he didn't actually witness it, but he heard the loud whump of metal against iron, the tinkling of broken glass. He spun around to see a low-slung black Porsche convertible pulling back from inside the gate. The woman behind the wheel then sped forward striking the gate again. This time it buckled and the hydraulic mechanism controlling movement opened the gates enough so that the vehicle was wedged into the opening. The woman accelerated, the motor growled in loud agitation, but the Porsche refused to move forward.

Finally, the woman leapt out of the car. Her long hair was pulled back in a ponytail. She wore white jeans and a blue denim shirt. From the photos he'd seen on the Internet, he recognized Elin Danielsen, Alexei Markov's mistress. She yelled something Tree couldn't understand, looking frustrated and angry. Then she climbed onto the hood of the car, using the windshield to balance herself.

At that moment, Valentin appeared, sweating and looking agitated. He yelled at Elin, and then tried to pull her off the car. But she pulled away, scurried along the hood, and jumped to the pavement outside the gate. Valentin was right behind her, grabbing her and yanking her around.

Tree said, "Hey, that's enough."

Both combatants appeared surprised to see him. Tree said, "Leave her alone."

Instead of doing what he was told, Valentin just smiled and shook his head. He released Elin and came toward him. He heard Elin say in English, "Valentin, don't—"

Valentin didn't pay any attention. Tree noticed something in Valentin's hand, heard the crunch of Valentin's foot against the dirt, a fleeting thought about the speed at which Valentin seemed to be moving, his arm raised.

Then, as they were wont to do these days, the stars exploded everywhere, followed by an intense flash of pain.

And right on cue, everything turned black.

17

Heaven was inside a wind tunnel.

That was the first thing that struck Tree the next time he was able to be struck by anything. Curious, he thought. Why would Heaven be in a wind tunnel? It didn't make any sense. But then little about Heaven did make sense, when he thought about it. After all, who would ever let him into Heaven?

Of course, the howling wind tunnel could be an indication of something else.

It might indicate he was not in Heaven.

Tree's eyes fluttered open to a view of blood-red water. And the wind blowing. He wondered how the water had turned to blood. Was it his blood?

Then the pain returned, exploding through his head, as though someone inside his skull was ramming a hot poker into his brain. He wanted to hold his head to stop the pain, only he couldn't move his hands. They appeared to be tied behind him.

Now he came to the realization he was in a wicker chair on a pool deck. The wicker chair was positioned so that it overlooked water, the wind gusting around him. The water became a deeper crimson, containing streaks of gold. A lovely Sanibel Island sunset was in progress. There was nothing like a Sanibel sunset, he decided. People came from all over the world to see this, and here it was right in front of him. But his head hurt so badly, and he was tied to a chair not knowing where he was, so it was hard to enjoy the beauty unfolding before him.

As he tried to process all this, the guy in his skull continued to stab at his brain tissue with the hot poker. Then his stomach abruptly turned, and he strained forward as best he could to throw up green bile that splattered across his knees onto the pool deck.

"Please do not vomit on my swimming pool, Mr. Callister," an accented voice behind him said. The voice did not sound unduly upset that Tree was sitting there tied to a wicker chair throwing up. He bent forward again, heaving up more bile.

The voice materialized into the stout form of Alexei Markov in linen shorts, flip flops, a plain white shirt fluttering in the breeze. Alexei held a cigar. Tree wondered how Judy, the wife who hated those awful reporters who smoked, could marry a guy who smoked cigars.

Tree thought of asking Alexei about that, but the pain was too intense. It was easier just to sit there and let the wind blow around him and watch the sun drawn relentlessly into oblivion. Kind of like himself, Tree thought; an aging gent in his sunset years sinking into extinction, helped along by a throbbing head and a cigar-smoking Russian who tied him to a chair.

"You are fortunate. This is Florida. Instead of a blow to the head, you might have received a bullet. But, thankfully where I come from we still prefer clubs to guns."

"You might tell your man Valentin not to assault women in front of your house," Tree said.

Alexei took a long puff on his cigar, placed it on the edge of a nearby table, and then stepped behind the chair and fumbled with the twist ties binding Tree's wrists. "I guess you are not too much of a threat to the neighborhood after all, Mr. Callister."

A moment later, Tree's hands were free. He leaned forward, finally able to hold his head in his hands. Not that it did much good, other to ascertain that there was a big lump but no blood.

Meanwhile, Alexei Markov straightened and returned to the table where he retrieved the smoldering cigar. He took another puff as he moved to position himself in front of the huddled Tree. "Now the question becomes this: what were you doing in front of my house?"

Through the searing pain in his head, Tree had the where-withal to say, "Everything's spinning. I can't remember."

"You can't remember why you came here?"

"Maybe I didn't know you lived here."

"So then why would you be standing out front?"

"Trying to help a woman who was being attacked," Tree said.

"A misunderstanding, nothing more," Markov said quietly. He took another puff on his cigar and sat back in his chair.

"This is a very curious situation, don't you think? My wife's ex-husband is found lurking around my house and he claims to have no idea how he got there."

"Maybe you shouldn't beat up women or hit ex-husbands over the head," Tree said.

"No woman was beaten, as you claim. A young lady was distraught. Valentin merely tried to calm her down so that we could help her."

"That's not how it looked to me," Tree said.

"However, you may have point when it comes to ex-husbands. I will chat with Valentin. What do they call it here? A teachable moment? Yes, that's what this is. A teachable moment. Be more careful with trespassing ex-husbands."

Alexei took another contemplative puff on his cigar. "I am coming to the unavoidable conclusion, Mr. Callister, that you are either very stupid or very foolish. I'm not sure which."

"It depends on what day you get me," Tree said. He lifted his head up. The movement created a drizzle of white pain. He clenched his teeth and squinted through it, trying to get a better look at Alexei. "Is Judy here?"

Alexei took his time drawing on the cigar before he said, "You can't remember why you come here, but you remember my wife's name."

"That's the kind of memory I have," Tree said. "Of course, it helps that I was married to her."

"Yes, I am reminded of that sad fact all too often since arriving on Sanibel."

"Is she here?"

"No."

"Now that I'm here, I thought I'd say hello."

"I'm sure she will be relieved to have missed you. Meantime, I take the liberty of using your cellphone to call your current wife. She is on the way here to bring you home. You should not be driving in your condition."

"I'm all right," Tree lied.

Tree rose uncertainly to his feet. He took a couple of tentative steps and then stumbled. Markov caught him, losing his cigar in the process.

"See what you do?" he said. "That was very expensive cigar."

"I'll bet you can afford it," Tree said.

"Aha." He seemed pleased as he helped Tree sit down again. "So you know about me. Great detective work? Or a visit to Google?"

"What I don't understand is why the U.S. government let you into the country," Tree said.

"That is because you do not know the truth of me. You see only fabrications, lies."

"You mean the dead wives and girlfriends?"

Markov ignored the dig. "You do not see things the United States government sees—the things your former wife sees."

"I wonder if Elin Danielsen still sees them after her encounter with Valentin."

Markov paused, a sign that jibe had found its mark. He recovered with a slight smile. "However, even though I am honest businessman, very successful, obviously, I did not get that way by being the nicest guy in the world. I remind you again, I am not a man you want to make unhappy."

"Do I make you unhappy, Alexei?"

"You make me sad, Mr. Callister. Sad at seeing the state you are in, sad that my beautiful wife wasted so much time with someone as inconsequential as you."

Valentin appeared. Tree looked at him and said, "Valentin, where have you been? Outside beating up women? Cracking more heads?"

Valentin ignored him and addressed Markov with guttural-sounding words that made no sense to Tree. Alexei nodded and turned to his guest. "Your wife has arrived."

The cavalry to the rescue, Tree thought.

18

A concussion, said the emergency room doctor, a young man named Rayhmond Noori, fresh-faced, ink-black hair perfectly cut, not old enough, as far as Tree was concerned, to drive let alone fix his throbbing head.

The brain is like gelatin, the youthful doctor continued. A violent blow causes the gelatin to slap back and forth crashing against the skull's inner walls.

A concussion.

All that knocking around, young Dr. Noori went on, causes bleeding in the brain, and that can result in a number of bad things ranging from confusion and drowsiness to death.

The chemicals in his brain had been jarred, the doctor further advised. It would take a week or so for them to return to normal. Maybe longer. In the meantime, Tree should take it easy. Refrain from any rough stuff.

Freddie agreed that was a very good idea. "What I can't understand is what you were doing there in the first place," she said as she drove him home from Lee Memorial Hospital, a place where he had spent far too much time in the last few years.

"I'm not sure," Tree said. "I may be experiencing memory loss. What I do remember is driving my car there. We have to get it back."

"Don't worry about your Beetle. Skye drove it home."

"Pat drove my car home?"

"You remember she prefers to be called Skye."

"I'm not allowed to forget."

"I brought her with me."

"Saved by two wives."

"I'm beginning to think it may take a platoon of wives to save you from yourself," Freddie said. "Speaking of your wives, was Judy there?"

"I don't think so, but my brain is in such a fog right now, I can't think straight."

"There are those who would say that's a perpetual condition," Freddie said.

"But not you," Tree said.

"Never crossed my mind."

When they got back to Andy Rosse Lane, the Beetle was in the drive, Pat in the kitchen heating up the lasagna she had picked up at Fresh Market. She was already into the wine, anxious to know if Tree was all right.

"When I was at the *Sun-Times* we did a takeout on concussions, mostly about kids, but it applied to adults, too," Pat said, her voice slurring. "I mean you could end up dead, right? These athletes, they're killing themselves, every time someone hits them. It's crazy. I used to go out with this Chicago Black Hawks guy? This was before I met Tree, of course. I was just a kid, doing some modelling around Chicago. He was crazy, this guy. A center. Or a left winger? I can't remember, but crazy, and when he abused certain substances, and I'm not saying anything specific here, he became violent. I couldn't deal with it. But he was cute, this guy. Can't even remember his name now. Talk about memory loss. But I do remember—well, I remember a few things about him I shouldn't talk about—but I do remember he was cute. Crazy but cute."

"So you ran off and married a safe, sane guy like Tree," Freddie said.

"Are you kidding?" Pat grimaced. "That wasn't safe or sane. That was a *mistake*." She reached out and touched Tree's arm. "Sorry, Tree, I don't mean to offend you, but it was a mistake, right? Should I even be talking like this? Probably not, right? But hey, we did get married, and here we are together again all these years later, me more or less on the run from yet another a-hole, excuse my French. It's come to that, hasn't it? At least Tree wasn't going to kill me." She looked at him. "You weren't, were you, Tree? You weren't trying to kill me?"

"No, Pat," Tree said patiently. "I wasn't trying to kill you."

"I guess when I think about it, you weren't a bad guy, compared to some of the other a-holes out there, excuse my French. I was probably a trifle rash when I took off, and I was the one who left, no denying that, with that jerk Bobby. I mean he wasn't even that great an editor, was he?"

"Bobby Bronsky was the guy who hired me at the *Sun-Times*," Tree said. "I liked him."

"You liked him? You liked Bobby Bronsky?"

"Whatever happened to him, anyway?"

"Who knows? Who cares?" said Pat. "You're too forgiving, Tree. That's your problem. You're too nice a guy. I suppose if I had it to do over again, I might have given us more of a chance than I did. Would you have liked that, Tree? Would you have liked me to stick around or were you sort of relieved when I disappeared with Bobby?"

That's exactly what he was—more or less. But he didn't want to say anything. "Listen," Tree said, "right now, I can't even remember how I got to that house today, let alone something that happened so long ago. We've both moved on. The past is the past. Whatever happened, it led me to Freddie, and I would not have wanted to miss that for the world."

"Me neither," Freddie affirmed.

Pat shifted her gaze to Freddie, her eyes suddenly welling with tears. "Freddie, you're a goddess, you really are. When I got here, I was really prepared to hate you. After all, you married my husband. I know, I know, I left him and all that. But he was my husband, at least for a while, and here you were this ageless beauty, and I guess I was kind of jealous and was just prepared to hate your guts."

"Hey, it's all right, Skye," Freddie said gently.

"But I love you, I truly do," Pat continued, her voice breaking. "You're so kind and wonderful, and Tree is so lucky to have you. Meanwhile, my life has turned to total crap. I've wandered around getting myself mixed up with every a-hole, excuse my French, imaginable, and now here I am running from a really major a-hole who is trying to kill me and the Palm Beach police are charging me and throwing me in jail, and I am such a total loser, I really am."

She said something else but it was lost in an explosion of tears. Freddie rose and embraced the weeping Pat. Or Skye, Tree thought, sitting there, his brain in a fog, viewing the spectacle of his fourth wife attempting to console his inconsolable third wife.

19

Freddie got Pat into bed in the guest bedroom and then came into the kitchen as Tree finished rinsing the dinner dishes and putting what was left of the lasagna into the fridge. Freddie looked at the empty chardonnay bottles lined up on the counter for recycling and groaned, "She drank all my wine."

"There was a time when Pat would cheerfully drink most of the reporters in the newsroom under the table, including me."

"Those hard-drinking Chicago newspaper days."

"Back then, men couldn't decide whether they wanted to drink with Pat or sleep with her."

"What about you? Which did you prefer?"

"I went one step further. I was crazy enough to marry her—despite ample warnings."

"Oh, yeah? Who warned you?"

"Rex, among others."

"Careful. The last wife he warned you about, he tried to marry."

"He liked Kelly, obviously. I don't think he ever liked Pat."

"She's clearly hurting—and I think she's a little regretful about the two of you."

"All these wives who now say they wish they were still married to me," Tree said.

"As long as you don't listen to them," Freddie said.

"Are you kidding?" He took her in his arms.

She hugged against him. "How are you feeling?"

"Like someone hit me in the head this afternoon," Tree said.

"That's understandable," Freddie said.

"I'm more concerned about how you are feeling about all these women elbowing their way into our lives, particularly when you're going through all this stuff with Dayton's."

"Don't worry about Dayton's," she said. "That's business. I can handle that."

"What about ex-wives?"

"I suppose if I'm being honest, I'm not sure how I feel. On the one hand, I'm trying to hang onto a sense of humor about it, and just shake my head over all the craziness. On the other hand, Rex is in jail accused of murdering his fiancée, your ex-wife, and that's not at all funny."

"No, it isn't," Tree said.

"On occasion, I'm feeling a trifle overwhelmed, but I'm dealing with it."

"I can't tell you how much I appreciate your patience," Tree said.

"What can I do?" Freddie said. "I can't have you getting another divorce. Think of how that would look."

"The scandal," Tree said. He kissed her mouth.

"You would be getting into Mickey Rooney territory." She kissed him back.

His cellphone vibrated in his pocket. "Damn," he said.

"You'd better see who it is," Freddie said.

It was Tommy Dobbs. Tree groaned. "What's up, Tommy?"

"Sorry to bother you so late, Mr. Callister. But I thought under the circumstances I'd better give you a call."

"What circumstances?"

"I've found out some stuff about Kelly Fleming that should interest you."

Through the fuzz in his brain, Tree remembered asking Tommy to do exactly that. "Okay," he said. "What did you find out?"

"I talked to some people in Chicago, just trying to pick up anything I could about Kelly. You know she was dumped at WBBM-TV, don't you?'

Did he know that? Yes, of course. His brain wasn't that fried. "It happened some time ago," Tree said. "Her ratings were down."

"That's the excuse they used, but I talked to Kim Doyle at the *Sun-Times*. He covers television for the paper. He told me there was more to it."

"What?" Tree demanded.

"It had something to do with the death of Miranda Hardy."

"Miranda Hardy?"

"The Illinois senator's wife. Senator John Hardy."

"Sure. I know who he is."

"Miranda woke up one morning in Chicago about a year ago, drove to Grant Park, parked the car, pulled a gun out of the glove compartment, and shot herself."

"I don't understand. What's a senator's wife got to do with this?"

"Everyone was speculating as to why this beautiful woman who seemed to have everything would commit suicide. Her husband was devastated, as you might imagine. In an interview, he said Miranda had been fighting depression for years."

"I remember something about this," Tree said. "But what's the point?"

"The point is, Mr. Callister, it wasn't long before the rumors started up."

"What rumors?"

"Talk that it wasn't necessarily only the depression that caused Miranda Hardy to take her own life. There were other contributing factors."

"Like what?"

"Like an affair she was having."

"With who, Tommy?"

"Kim Doyle and a lot of other people in the Chicago media believe she was having an affair with Kelly."

"Kelly Fleming?" Tree couldn't keep the note of incredulousness out of his voice.

"They were lovers, Mr. Callister."

"Lovers?" The inside of his head felt like thick porridge.

"Kelly Fleming and Miranda Hardy." Tommy, showing impatience with Tree's continuing failure to connect the dots.

It was raining on the porridge in Tree's brain. He struggled through the rain.

Tommy continued. "Kim says everything was hushed up and Kelly left town shortly afterward."

"Did he know where she went?"

"Here. Sanibel Island."

Tree wondered how much Rex might have known about any of this.

Tommy went on. "So now that Kelly is dead, everyone in Chicago is chasing the story, how Miranda's suicide fits into Kelly's murder."

"How does it fit in, Tommy?"

"That's what my paper wants me to find out. What do you think, Mr. Callister? Any ideas?"

"It doesn't fit." Tree's head was hurting more than ever. "This is crazy."

Freddie was sitting up, tense, watching him carefully.

"I know how you're feeling." Tommy said. "Having been married to her and everything. But when you stop to think about it, it does kind of make sense. I mean, it helps explain why Miranda committed suicide and why Kelly left Chicago so fast and how she ended up on Sanibel Island."

How could it possibly make sense? Tree thought. How could a suicide in Chicago lead to a murder on Sanibel Island? But then nothing made sense lately. He was at the Mad Hatter's tea party, married to all the guests, and he had a headache.

20

Tree's headache was gone. He felt totally refreshed as he bounded out of bed. A Philips radio on a nightstand next to the bed emitted the scratchy sound of Marilyn Monroe singing "Let's Make Love." Where did that radio come from? Tree wondered.

A nearby door opened and a small woman wrapped in a white towel emerged from the bathroom, tousled blond hair, a bright, round face, smiling provocatively, devastatingly lovely.

"Well, what do you know?" she said in a breathless little-girl voice. "You've got nothing on but the radio."

Tree looked down at himself. Sure enough, he was naked. "I shouldn't be like this in front of you," he said.

"Why not?" the blonde replied. "This is what you've always wanted, isn't it? Just the two of us and no clothes."

"What's wrong with me?" Tree said. "Why am I still thinking like this?"

"Because of all the women you've met in your life, all the experiences you've had, there is still nothing quite like me, right? I'm lodged in your mind forever, Tree, always available."

"But I don't want you," Tree protested.

"Don't be silly," she replied. "I'm here, aren't I? You must still want me. You'll always desire me, you see. I'm the one who will never disappoint you or betray you."

"I've failed at so many relationships," Tree said sadly.

"You never fail with me," she said. "That's why you keep me around. The others come and go, but not me. I'm eternal, don't you see? Always there for you, no matter what."

Tree said, "Would you like to know what's always amazed me about the fascination with you?"

She grinned impishly. "Uh-oh. Don't tell me you're going to get all intellectual trying to explain this. Don't you get it, Tree? None of this comes from the head. It comes from here..."

She made a playful grab for him. He yelped and jumped away. "Hey, stop that."

She giggled. "That's what it's all about, nothing else."

"What I started to say, what intrigues me, is that none of your movies are memorable, but you are."

She pouted. "My movies aren't so bad."

"No matter what you think of them, they're all but forgotten today. But everyone knows who you are."

"They know I'm Norma Jeane?"

"Most people don't even know your real name. Even so, you're an icon; your face is everywhere."

She plumped herself down on the edge of the bed, the towel beginning to slip. "Being an icon ain't all it's cracked up to be, I'm here to tell you. Not when it comes to relationships. Come to think of it, I didn't do any better than you. I guess the two of us have that in common."

"That's not true," Tree said.

"No? Listen, I messed up three marriages: a small-town loser, a baseball player, and a playwright. Actually, the playwright might have worked, if only I'd been able to keep my hands off Yves Montand."

"If only we all had resisted temptation, we might have saved ourselves a lot of trouble," Tree said.

"I can't disagree with you there. But hey, I was young and a little crazy, and horny, too, I suppose, and it certainly was fun. It was always fun at the time, wasn't it, Tree? It's only later that the regrets start to crowd in."

"Wake up, Tree, wake up."

The blonde started, her mouth dropping open, turning. "What was that?"

"Tree, wake up, Tree."

"Who's that?" the blonde demanded.

"It's my wife," Tree said.

She issued another sigh, this one resigned. "At some point they always show up, don't they? But they're no match for me. They think they are, but they aren't."

"No," Tree said. "I love my wife. I love the reality of her, I do."

"Tree!" Freddie's voice calling. "Tree, wake up!"

"You'll be back," the blonde said.

The towel dropped away. All that she had on was the radio, Marilyn Monroe singing. The blonde purred, "The fantasy, Tree, it's always better than the reality."

"Tree, please wake up," Freddie called.

"Always, Tree. Always so much better..."

Tree blinked awake and looked up to see Freddie hovering over him.

"I couldn't wake you up. I was worried."

"What's wrong?" Tree said, trying to sit up.

"Nothing," Freddie said. "It's still early. With that concussion, I'm supposed to wake you up every few hours."

"I had this strange dream," Tree said.

"It's the concussion," Freddie said.

"It's my life," Tree said. "It's my crazy, misspent life."

"Don't be so hard on yourself," Freddie said. "You are going to get through this."

No, Tree thought. No matter what happens, nobody gets through, not even gorgeous blondes with nothing on but the radio.

21

Reality brought his headache back. Not as bad as the night before, but still throbbing away as he stepped under the shower. The rain inside his skull had ceased; the porridge had mostly disappeared so that his mind felt as clear as his muddled brain ever felt these days—clear enough to struggle with the implications of what Tommy Dobbs had told him over the phone the night before.

Kelly had been involved in a relationship with a senator's wife. That was possible he supposed, although nothing that occurred during their marriage gave him any indication Kelly might be inclined that way. But then what did he know? Very little about anything as it turned out, and besides, they were a long time ago, and lots could have changed since then.

He turned so that the spray from the rain-forest shower head punched into his back, sending currents of welcome warmth through his body. That's better, he thought. If he could not quite conquer the world today, he could at least stagger through it.

Certainly, Miranda Hardy's suicide might explain Kelly's unexpected presence on Sanibel in the company of Rex Baxter. Her Chicago broadcast career at an end, her lover dead of a self-inflicted gunshot wound, and there was Rex, the puppy dog in love, to whisk her away to an island paradise. What she hadn't expected was Rex so in love that he would ask her to marry him—pressure her to marry him? Perhaps the pressure was too much. Kelly couldn't go through with a marriage to a man who was good enough to get her out of Chicago, but not appropriate for a more demanding commitment.

But while all that might explain Kelly's actions, it did not explain why anyone would kill her. Unless, of course...

No, he wouldn't go there. He would stay away from that.

He turned off the shower and stepped out onto the bath mat, grabbing for one of the big, fluffy towels with which Freddie had blessed their marriage.

Then, before he could stop it, the thought forced itself through the muddle inside his head:

Unless, of course, Rex murdered Kelly.

There. Out in the open. Well, not quite. It hadn't left his lips, thankfully. He kept most of his crazy thoughts locked inside his addled head where they belonged.

But what if Kelly told Rex about her affair with Miranda Hardy, admitted that she did not love him, loved the dead Miranda instead?

If that were the case, then Rex certainly would have had motive. Wouldn't he?

No, he thought. No, no, no. None of this wild thinking had any basis in reality. Whatever the possible motivation, Rex wasn't a killer. However broken up he might have been over the end of his relationship with Kelly, he still would have loved her, and would not have wanted any harm to come to her.

But if not Rex, then who? Who else would have any reason to murder Kelly?

He was standing there, thinking this, holding that big fluffy towel when the door opened and Freddie stuck her head inside.

"Are you all right?"

"Fine," Tree mumbled.

"T. Emmett Hawkins wants to see us as soon as possible," Freddie said.

———

"I've heard from ADA Lee Bixby," Hawkins said. "As is usual in these matters, he is offering a deal."

"What kind of deal?" Freddie inquired. They were once again seated in Hawkins's downtown Fort Myers law office.

Hawkins perched in his usual easy chair, his soft hands resting on either arm, looking fresh and alert and ready to pounce.

"I will get to that in a moment," Hawkins said. "In a nutshell, their case appears to amount to this: that when Kelly Fleming returned to Rex's house to gather up her things, Rex confronted her. An argument ensued that resulted in him assaulting her. When she attempted to leave, he followed her out to the pool deck where he continued his assault, eventually knocking her down and hitting her head against the tiles of the pool deck."

"Good grief," Freddie gasped.

Hawkins continued, "ADA Bixby asserts that when Rex realized Kelly was dead, he hid her body in the pool house and then did his best to clean up the evidence on the deck. After he was finished, he drove to the chamber, spent time there before going to your place with some notion of establishing an alibi and giving himself time to think about how to dispose of the body. However, he forgot that Brittany Pools was coming to clean the pool. She found the body thus ending any plans Rex had for covering up his crime."

"And they have the evidence to back this?" Freddie, again.

"ADA Bixby assures me that they do, although so far he is not revealing exactly what he does have. He says, however, that this is the case he plans to take to a grand jury, presuming they will return a true bill. In other words, he will indict Rex for murder and put him away for life."

"But you mentioned a deal," Freddie reminded him.

"ADA Bixby is willing to reduce the murder charge to one that would require Rex to plead guilty to involuntary manslaughter; that is, he acted with culpable negligence, and Kelly died as a result."

"But Rex didn't do it," Tree said.

"I reminded ADA Bixby of that," Hawkins said dryly. "Unfortunately, he disagrees with our assessment."

"How much time would Rex spend in jail?" Tree asked.

"Conviction on a manslaughter charge means the judge would possibly sentence Rex to fifteen years in prison."

"At his age that's a life sentence," Tree said.

"Precisely," Hawkins said.

"That's not much of a deal," Tree said. "In fact, it's no deal at all."

"That's what they're offering, I'm afraid," Hawkins said.

"So now what?" Freddie asked.

"I believe you are both familiar with the process. I will consult with my client. I suspect, as you suspect, he will reject the ADA's offer. Under the circumstances, there's absolutely no reason to accept it. The ADA will then move the proceeding before a grand jury."

"Any chance the grand jury will decline to return this true bill?" Freddie again.

"Anything is possible, of course. Their case does seem weak from what I can see. It all appears to be based on circumstantial evidence. No one actually witnessed Rex commit the crime the state is accusing him of. But having said that, as you know, the prosecution usually gets what it wants from a grand jury, and what the prosecution wants is a murder indictment."

Hawkins raised his hands off the armrests and formed them into a tent through which he peered at Tree. "Once again, I must stress that the more you can do to demonstrate the real killer is on the loose and not residing in the Lee County jail, the better."

"As they say in law enforcement," Tree said, "I'm investigating a number of leads."

"What does that mean?"

"Before I say too much, I'd better talk to Rex."

Hawkins collapsed his tent and issued an impatient sigh. "Just be careful what you say to him," he advised. "The authorities are undoubtedly recording any visitor conversations."

22

Rex looked paler than ever on the over-bright television screen, and somehow older, as though imprisonment had brought out his true age, the age he had managed to disguise for so many years.

"What happened to you?" he demanded when he saw Tree.

"What makes you think anything happened?"

"You want me to be honest with you?"

"I hate it when you're honest with me," Tree said.

"You look awful."

"Do I?"

"Of course, that's just me being honest, and overlooking the fact I'm locked in a cage and look pretty ghastly myself."

"You look fine," Tree said.

"Quit lying and tell me what happened."

"Someone hit me over the head. I guess I don't bounce back like I used to."

"You've never bounced back," Rex said. "Let's face it, Tree, you're not exactly the action-hero type."

"I'm beginning to think you may be right."

"Getting conked on the head. Was this in connection with your Free Rex Baxter campaign?"

"It could have been, I'm not sure," Tree said.

"Well, don't get yourself killed on my account."

"Hey," Tree said. "If I'm going to get myself killed on anyone's account, it's going to be yours."

"Hawkins said you wanted to talk to me."

"You wouldn't be happy if I just came for a visit?"

"Plenty of time to visit once you get me out of here," Rex said.

"I'm glad you think I can get you out," Tree said.

"I've had a chance to ponder the notion—a lot of chances in fact." Rex fixed a wan smile. "Let's put it this way: as improbable as it seems, you are just about my only hope of getting out of this mess."

"Hawkins believes the prosecution's case is weak."

"I'm paying him to say that," Rex replied. "I'd prefer not to take any chances. If you could prove I'm innocent before the trial, that would be the best."

"What do you know about a woman named Miranda Hardy?"

Rex looked at him blankly.

"Apparently when she was in Chicago Kelly had an affair with Miranda Hardy. Senator John Hardy's wife."

"Yes, I know who she is," Rex said.

"Miranda committed suicide."

Tree waited for a surprised expression to cross Rex's face. There was none. "Do you know anything about that?"

Rex said, "The question I have is, How do you know?"

"Great detective work on my part?"

"I doubt it," Rex said.

"You remember Tommy Dobbs?"

"That kid from the *Island Reporter*?"

"He's working in Chicago now for the *Sun-Times*. He did some digging."

A look of irritation crossed Rex's face. "I don't want some reporter sticking his nose into that stuff."

"He's trying to help us."

"That isn't going to help, believe me."

"Look, when I confronted Kelly in the parking lot, she actually said something about this. At least I believe she did."

"What did she say?"

"She asked me if I ever got involved in something that was intriguing at first, but it turned out to be nothing more than an experiment, that you ended up paying a big price for. I thought she was talking about you, but she may have been referring to her affair with Miranda."

"I knew Kelly had had a relationship with Miranda Hardy. But I can't understand how you think it makes any difference to what's happened here."

"I'm not sure it does—until I know all the facts."

"Look, not that it makes any difference to anything, but by the time I ran into Kelly, Miranda was dead. The subject never came up until we were back on Sanibel Island."

"What did Kelly say about it?"

"For her it was kind of an experiment. She had just been downsized from WBBM, she was feeling pretty lousy. I guess Miranda sort of came onto her. Kelly was intrigued enough to let it play out for a time."

"How did Kelly feel about the suicide?"

"Devastated, she said. Like she said to you, she thought it was a fling. But Miranda took it a whole lot more seriously."

"Miranda committed suicide because of Kelly?"

"That's what Miranda's husband thinks."

"Senator Hardy?"

Rex nodded. "Hardy blames her for his wife's death. That's why Kelly wanted to get out of town for a time."

"Why she came to Sanibel."

"One of the reasons, yeah," Rex said.

"And you were fine with that?"

"Like I said, I didn't hear the details until we were on Sanibel, but I thought there had been other relationships. She was an attractive woman with a high profile, how would there not be someone? I just didn't realize it was another woman until she told me." He allowed the ghost of a smile. "Besides, as you know, I had ulterior motives. I wanted her close so I could love her."

"But not to kill her."

"No, of course not."

"Even though she said she didn't love you."

"She never said she didn't love me," Rex said. "She just said she didn't want to marry me."

On the TV monitor, Tree could see the tears in his old friend's eyes. "Hey," he said. "It's going to be all right."

"This could turn out to be many things," Rex said, his voice breaking, "but it's never going to be all right."

———————

Todd Jackson phoned Tree as he reached the parking lot outside the Lee County jail. "Just checking in," Todd said.

"I'm just leaving the jail now," Tree said.

"How's he doing?"

"He doesn't look so great in an orange jump-suit, I can tell you that," Tree said. "But I guess you can say he's hanging in there."

"Look, no reason to raise any alarms, but I just came out of a board of directors meeting at the chamber over here on the island," Todd said.

"Problems?"

"Not at the moment," Todd said. "But as you can imagine, nobody's talking about anything else."

"I don't have to imagine," Tree said.

"Actually, that's not quite true. There is one other topic of discussion."

"What's that?"

"My way of telling you how sorry I am to hear about what's happened to Freddie."

"That's out, is it?"

"I'm afraid so. The story is those sons of bitches she brought into Dayton's have now turned on her."

"Freddie's surprisingly philosophical about it, I must say."

"She's a brilliant woman. She'll bounce back. Give her my best will you?"

"I'll do that. Much appreciated. Listen, Todd. Who did the cleanup at Rex's place when the police were finished?"

"That was my Sanibel Biohazard crew," Todd said.

"You didn't notice anything, did you?"

"I'm not even sure why we got called out," Todd said. "Whoever killed Kelly did a pretty good job cleaning up. I think the forensic guys found blood traces between the stones, but for us there wasn't much."

"What about in the pool house?"

"Some blood in there on the floor where the body had been, but not much," Todd said.

"Okay," Tree said.

"I'm really worried about Rex," Todd said.

"I know. We all are."

"You're going to be able to get him off, aren't you, Tree?"

"I'm doing everything I can," Tree said. "The district attorney's office has offered a deal, but it's crap. It would mean Rex would spend the rest of his life in prison."

"You're the Sanibel Sunset Detective, right?" Todd's voice was full of hope. "To everyone's surprise, you've actually pulled a few rabbits out of the hat in the past and solved some cases. You've even been on television. You can do this, Tree. I know you can."

"I hope you're right, Todd," Tree said.

"I've got faith in you, pal." Then Todd paused before he said, "He's innocent, right?" Todd sounded anxious. "Rex didn't do this, did he?"

"Todd."

"Sorry, but like I say, everyone's talking, everyone's speculating. There are some people around here who think he could be guilty."

"Well, he's not," Tree said.

"Of course he isn't," Todd hurried on. "It's ridiculous to even think like that. But listen, Tree, there's some movement among members of the board to suspend Rex pending the outcome of this whole situation."

"Is that going to happen?"

"I hope not. I'm twisting some arms, trying to head it off. You know, the guy's innocent until proven guilty, that sort of thing. But, of course, everyone's worried about the island's image and what this whole murder thing could do to tourism."

"I don't believe it," Tree said. "Wait. Let me correct that. I do believe it."

"Not to put any pressure on you or anything, but the sooner you can prove Rex innocent, the better."

Tree pocketed his cellphone and closed his eyes, leaning against the Beetle. His head was hurting again. He wanted to lie down and forget about everything. But he couldn't. He had to save his oldest friend.

All he had to do was figure out how to do it.

23

When Tree got back to Andy Rosse Lane, he found Pat in the kitchen dressed in a pair of Freddie's shorts and one of her T-shirts. She was staring at the coffee machine as if willing it to make coffee for her. It wasn't working.

"What is the deal with this thing?" she said, training bleary eyes on Tree.

"Here, let me," he said.

"You're a saint," Pat said.

"Where's Freddie?"

"She said she had a meeting and to tell you she'd be back in a couple of hours. Is something wrong? There seems to be things going on here I don't know about."

"There's a lot going on, that's for sure," Tree said. He turned on the tap and filled the coffee pot with water.

"Like former wives turning up at the door and getting drunk," Pat said.

"How are you feeling?"

"Like a bag of hammers, as we used to say in the newsroom."

Tree poured the water into the top of the coffee maker while Pat retreated a few feet to let him work.

"Did I make a fool of myself last night?"

Tree said, "We like flavored coffee, hazelnut in this case. Is that all right?"

"Sure, anything with caffeine in it, at this point," she said. "And you never answered my question."

"Did you make a fool of yourself?"

She grinned. "Okay, I get it. You don't have to answer. Freddie's lovely, incidentally, to put up with you and then all my crap."

"You kept telling her that last night," Tree said.

"Oh, no," Pat said. "I really did make a fool out of myself."

He served her the coffee down on the terrace. She sipped at it and nodded approvingly. "This is great. Thanks."

"So tell me about all your crap, Pat, what's going on?"

She groaned. "Where to begin?"

"Come on, you've never had any trouble talking about the various dramas in your life."

"Now don't be mean, Tree," she said, putting the coffee on the glass-topped table beside her. "My head hurts this morning."

"So does mine," Tree said. "Tell me what happened in Palm Beach."

"Tal Fiala happened. He's an awful rat."

"Is he really after you?"

"You think I'm making it up?"

"I don't know, Pat, you tell me."

"Skye. How many times do I have to remind you? I changed my name to Skye. You just do that to irritate me, Tree. You always did things to irritate me."

"There is a whole lot I could say in answer to that, but I'm not going to say anything. I'm going to wait patiently for you to quit dodging and tell me what's got you so frightened."

"All right," she said with a grimace. "I told you about these trumped-up charges, right?"

"You've been charged with defrauding a demented old lady," Tree said. "What do they say you stole? Was it five million dollars?"

The grimace on Pat's face deepened. "I didn't take her money, I didn't defraud Doris Bermann. How could I defraud her? She's my friend. Like I said before, I've known her forever, since Chicago."

"Okay, I know all that. But what's happened since I was in Palm Beach? When I was there, you were introducing me to Tal. He didn't seem interested enough to even show up when you got out of jail. You had to go chasing after him."

"I didn't *chase* after him."

"Now you're running away from him. Why? What's happened? What's he done?"

"Tal and I were dating when I took on Doris's power of attorney, right? I don't know how I always fall for these jerk men, Tree. What is it about me, anyway?"

"Since I am one of the jerks, I'm hardly in a position to say."

"Well, you're beginning to look like less of a jerk."

"You were dating Tal," Tree said, trying to get her back on track. "So what happened? He talked you into letting him be the attorney for Doris's estate."

She gave him a surprised look. "How did you know?"

"Lucky guess," he said. "Did he have access to Doris's accounts?"

"I mean, he was her attorney and I was in love—thought I was in love—so of course, like an idiot, I trusted the guy."

"So now the five million is gone from her estate. The district attorney has indicted you both, but recently, the DA's office arranged to have a little talk with you. Have I got it right?"

"Yes, but how do you know all this stuff?"

"What are they offering?"

"Tal is the bad guy, after all," she went on. "He took the money out of Doris's account. I didn't know anything about the Lamborghini. I mean, I knew he bought a Lamborghini, but I didn't know he used her money. I had no idea, honestly."

"So what are they offering you?"

"A reduced sentence if I testify against Tal."

"What's a reduced sentence mean?"

"Six months jail time, and then there would be three years' probation, and I'd have to give back the money they say I have."

"Do you have the money?"

"Are you kidding? I'm broke. Tal's got all the money."

"So now Tal's gotten wind of this deal, and he's threatening you."

"He's not threatening me," she said vehemently. "He's going to kill me if he gets his hands on me. As it turns out, this guy isn't someone you should fool around with. Like he's defended several organized-crime figures, as they call these guys in the newspapers, and these guys are friends of his and probably only too anxious to help him stay out of jail."

"Pat—Skye—how the blazes do you get yourself into these predicaments?"

"I should have stayed married to you," she said in a forlorn voice.

"No, no you shouldn't have. Getting rid of me was a smart move. It's the rest of it that's open to question."

"I'm a fool," she said. "An absolute fool, and now it's going to get me killed."

"Does he know where you are?"

She shook her head. "I'm hoping the last thing he'll figure is that I would run to my ex-husband."

"Except he knows you called me when you were arrested."

"I don't know, I don't know what he's thinking, but I'm scared, Tree, and I'm sorry to get you mixed up in this but I didn't know where else to turn."

"It's all right, Skye. You did the right thing coming here." A white lie if there ever was one.

"Oh, Tree, I know you can protect me, I know you can," she gushed.

Sure, he thought. No problem at all for the heroic Tree Callister. He would protect his third wife from a murderous lover, rescue his first wife from a fate worse than death at the hands of a Russian oligarch, and save his best friend from a life in prison. Good old Tree to the rescue.

The front door chimes sounded. Pat looked suddenly nervous. She said, "Are you expecting anyone?"

"No," Tree said. He got up and went across the terrace and climbed the steps leading to the kitchen. He crossed the living room and opened the front door. Judy, his first wife, stood on the threshold.

"May I come in?" she said.

"Yes, of course." Tree stepped away to allow her inside. Pat hovered behind him, a frown gathering. "What are you doing here?" she said to Judy.

Judy reacted with an expression approaching shock. "I might ask you the same question, Patricia."

"Skye," Pat said irritably. "I now call myself Skye."

"I'm not surprised," Judy said.

"What is that supposed to mean?" Pat demanded.

Tree addressed Judy. "I just made fresh coffee. Would you like some?"

Judy shook her head. "I heard what happened. I wanted to make sure you're all right."

"Nothing more than a sore head," Tree said.

"Alexei is furious, of course. Somehow, he blames me for you being at the house."

"Are you all right?"

"I'm fine, except now his suspicions have been aroused, and that's never a good thing."

"What's going on here?" Pat demanded.

"This is none of your business, Patricia. I would ask you to allow me to speak to Tree privately."

Pat arranged to look offended. "For your information, I've hired Tree to do some work for me, and I certainly don't like the idea of you distracting him."

Judy's head snapped back. "I'm distracting him?" She made the sort of harrumphing sound Tree hadn't heard since their marriage ended. "If I am, it's giving him some relief from your antics."

"*My antics*? Excuse me? I'd like to know what the hell you're talking about. *My antics*."

"Come on, Pat. Be serious. Everyone knows you are mentally disturbed."

"The Doris Day-imitation housewife thinks *I'm* mentally disturbed? Have you looked into a mirror lately? And incidentally, Doris Day is dead."

"That goes to show how little you know," Judy shot back. "Doris Day is not dead. She is very much alive."

"Okay, children, let's play nicely together," Tree said.

"Tree, tell Judy that Doris Day is dead."

"Skye," Tree continued in the sternest voice he was able to muster, "I need you to listen to me."

"Tell her, Tree."

Tree maneuvered himself directly in front of Pat so that her view of Judy was blocked. "Do me a favor and let me have a few minutes alone with Judy."

"Not until you tell her that Doris Day is dead." Pat's voice was tight.

"She's not dead, Pat."

Pat paused for a time and then said, "Sure, that's fine. I need to take a shower, anyway." She swirled away with a regal air into the guest bedroom and slammed the door.

Tree turned to the smoldering Judy. "Let's talk outside."

Judy said, "Yes, that's a good idea."

Tree guided her down to the terrace and sat her in the chair recently occupied by Pat. The doctor once again was in. The ineffective, stumblebum doctor was in way over his head. With Tree sitting facing her, Judy clasped her hands together, taking deep breaths.

"What is that woman doing here?"

"Pat's visiting from Palm Beach," Tree said.

"She's *visiting*? This woman who deserted you and ran off with another man, she's *visiting*? Isn't that the modern approach?"

"She's having some difficulties," Tree said, the biggest understatement of the day so far. "We're trying to help."

"All your troubled ex-wives," Judy said with a slight smile. "How can you keep up?"

"I'm asking myself the same question," Tree said. "What did Alexei say to you?"

"He said you had been snooping around the house, and that Valentin had hit you over the head."

"Because I tried to stop him from assaulting Elin."

"Tree, you shouldn't have done that."

"I should have allowed Valentin to assault your husband's mistress?"

"You shouldn't have been there in the first place."

"I had no idea that it was your house," Tree said. "I was following a woman named Brittany Pools."

Judy made a face. "Why would you be following Brittany?"

"You know her?"

"I know Alexei is sleeping with her, if that's what you mean."

"You're kidding," Tree said, not trying to hide his surprise.

"Why would I kid about something like that? I assume she went to the house knowing I wasn't there so he could screw her."

"What about Elin Danielsen?"

"Elin is a very a very jealous woman. I guess she thought she might find Alexei with Brittany. And I suppose she was right about that."

"I'm sorry, Judy."

"Don't be sorry. These are the things I have to do deal with. What I don't understand is why you were following Brittany."

"It's probably nothing more than wild coincidence, but Brittany found Kelly Fleming's body. When I went around to talk to her, Valentin showed up. The next thing, she was in her sports car driving over to your place."

"She also cleans our pools," Judy said. "In addition to her other duties."

"Is that how Alexei met her?"

"When she showed up to clean the pool? I suppose so, but really, I have no idea. These are not details he shares with me."

"If Elin is jealous of Brittany, what does she think of you?"

"She thinks she should be married to Alexei. She thinks I am in her way."

"Where is she now?"

"My understanding is that after what happened the other day, she has left the country."

"How do you feel about that?"

"Ambivalent, I suppose. She may have left Sanibel but she certainly hasn't left his life."

"You can't go back to Moscow."

"That envelope I gave you."

"I've still got it. Do you need it back?"

"Not for the moment. You didn't open it, did you?"

Tree shook his head. "No, of course not. Do you want to tell me what's in it?"

"It's the insurance Alexei won't do anything he's not supposed to."

"Are you sure that's enough?"

Before Judy had a chance to answer, Valentin came through the sliding doors from the kitchen, and started down to the terrace.

"I have come to take Mrs. Markov to her home," he announced in the kind of heavily-accented rumble expected from a Russian bodyguard.

Her face knotted in anger, Judy leapt to her feet. "Valentin, this is unacceptable. You must leave immediately."

"Please to come with me, Mrs. Markov," Valentin said.

"I am visiting with Mr. Callister. I will return home when I am good and ready. Now, leave."

For a guy the size of a refrigerator, Tree reflected later, Valentin sure could move fast when he had to. Tree couldn't remember him getting close enough to deliver that punch to the solar plexus. He couldn't remember the punch. However, he abruptly found himself sprawled on the ground, gasping, thinking that he wasn't doing so well against Russian thugs.

He was vaguely aware of Valentin grabbing Judy and wrestling her toward the stairs. Valentin stopped wrestling when another figure came rushing down the stairs.

It was Pat, aka Skye.

Pat would never have had a gun in her hand, Tree reflected. But Skye had one.

24

Pat's gun distracted Valentin enough so that Judy, breathing hard, could break away.

"I don't know what's going on here," Pat said to Valentin between gritted teeth, keeping the gun steady on him. "But honey, I think you should leave."

"You will not shoot me," Valentin said, trying to paste on a confident smile.

"Are you kidding? Honey, this is South Florida and you're trespassing, and I'm crazy. That's the sort of lethal combination that gets you killed in these parts. Just be lucky I'm feeling generous today, and haven't pulled the trigger. Now do as I say. Get the hell out."

Valentin kept his eyes trained on the gun as though trying to figure the odds of it going off in his direction. He must have decided the odds weren't worth it. Pat was absolutely right. He was in South Florida. Even a tough Russian thug could get himself shot here. He tried on another smile, this one not so confident. He turned to Judy.

"I will tell my boss," he said.

Judy, pale and trembling, didn't say anything. Valentin made his exit up the stairs and through the sliding glass doors. As soon as he was gone, Pat lowered the gun. Judy hurried over and embraced her, burying her head in Pat's shoulder and beginning to weep.

For a moment, Pat was taken aback, not quite sure what to do. Then she put her arms around Judy and hugged her. "Hey, everything's okay," Pat said in a soothing voice Tree seldom heard when they were married. "It's all good. All men are a-holes. Excuse my French."

Tree, collapsed on the pool deck, was ignored until he groaned trying to get to his feet. Then Pat broke her embrace with the sobbing Judy and said to Tree, "What's wrong with you?"

"I don't think I can get up."

"Oh, for goodness sake, Tree," Pat said. She put the gun on the glass-topped table and came over to help him. "Here we go," she said, struggling to lift him up. Judy arrived and together, they managed to get their former husband upright. Tree was bent over, gasping, experiencing the same white hot stomach pain that had previously assaulted his head.

"Where did you get that gun?" he said to Pat.

"What kind of question is that?" Pat said. "Who doesn't have a gun?"

"I don't," Tree said.

Pat said, "How can you live in Florida without a gun?"

———————

"I can't be sure if it's one or two broken ribs, we'd have to do an X-ray to know for certain," said young Dr. Rayhmond Noori, the same whipper snapper who had treated him before.

"Shouldn't we know that?" Tree said.

"It doesn't really make any difference. We used to tape up the rib cage, but we don't do that any longer."

"Why not?" Tree asked.

"Taping the patient doesn't allow him or her to breathe properly, and that can cause pneumonia, particularly in someone your age."

"My age," Tree said.

"Which reminds me," the doctor said. "This is the second time in a week you've been in here. I'm a little concerned about what you're doing to yourself."

"It has crossed my mind that I'm in here too often," Tree said.

"Do you mind if I ask what you do for a living?"

"I'm retired," said Tree.

The doctor just stared at him.

Tree said, "What should I do about my broken ribs."

"They will heal by themselves in the next six weeks or so. In the meantime I can put you on a pain medication, and let nature take its course."

"Any other advice?"

"No heavy breathing and, oh yeah, this is probably the best advice I can give you—stay out of trouble."

———

Freddie was waiting for Tree and his two former wives when they arrived back at Andy Rosse Lane. She helped Tree settle himself on the sofa in the living room and got him a Diet Coke. Judy and Pat fussed over him, one current wife and two exes working together to make him comfortable. Who would have guessed?

Judy filled Freddie in on what had happened on the terrace, full of praise for Skye's courageous intervention. Freddie took it all in with surprising equanimity. He waited for her, the law-biding citizen, to suggest the typical remedy for criminal-type behavior—calling the police. This was immediately rejected by the other two women.

"Honey, I'm under indictment in Palm Beach," Pat said. "If they get wind of me with a gun in Fort Myers, my goose is cooked."

"Really, Freddie, your impulse is the correct one," chimed in Judy, "but arresting Valentin doesn't help me at all; in fact, it only enrages Alexei without doing him any harm, and places me in even more jeopardy than I am in now."

"This Markov creep is planning to kill Judy," Pat said. "At least that's what we suspect he's got in mind." Then, not wanting to be left out of the killer boyfriend sweepstakes, she added, "On top of that, my boyfriend is trying to kill me."

"Which I'm sure is why Skye now carries a gun, right Skye?" added Judy.

"That is absolutely why," Pat agreed.

"In fact, Freddie," Judy added, "you are very unusual in this group."

"Yeah, your husband isn't trying to kill you," Pat said.

"I knew there was a good reason to marry this guy," Freddie said.

"You're so lucky, Freddie, you really are," Judy said. And then she burst into tears.

Pat wrapped her arm around her new friend. "Hey, we're going to get out of this. It's going to be all right."

Judy sniffled some more and said, "I don't know. It all seems so hopeless."

"Let's open some wine," Freddie suggested. "Things never look so bad after a glass of wine."

"Or two," added Pat.

Freddie rose and went into the kitchen, the two other women following, making noises about pitching in to help—the bonding of the wife with the ex-wives. Tree would have shaken his head in amazement, except his head was hurting almost as much as his ribs.

He settled back on the sofa, closing his eyes. That was better. The pain subsided in his head and concentrated on his ribs. His cellphone buzzed in his pocket. He gritted his teeth as his body informed him that even the simple act of retrieving his phone would cost him dearly.

It was T. Emmett Hawkins.

"I have informed ADA Bixby that we will not accept his plea offer," Hawkins said in a formal voice. "He has told me that he plans to take the indictment before a grand jury as early as possible. In the meantime, he says he will resist any further efforts to obtain bail for my client. Unfortunate, but not unexpected under the circumstances."

"I'm not sure whether this is good news or bad," Tree said.

"It is the typical unfolding of a homicide case in Florida," Hawkins said. "Lee Bixby is not at all surprised we rejected his plea offer; we also are not surprised he is taking the case to a grand jury. The wrench in the machinery of justice is you, Tree. You can change the otherwise unalterable course of this case by the simple act of finding the real killer."

"I'm working on it," Tree said.

"You keep saying that," Hawkins said. There was a note of disappointment in his smooth, southern voice. "Excuse me for saying so, but you've got to do more than simply work on it, as you say. You've got to come up with results, and you've got to come up with them quickly."

25

The Tree Wives Club, as Tree had privately dubbed the group, had convened down on the terrace. Freddie had opened a second bottle of chardonnay.

Tree watched them through the kitchen window, marveling yet again at the curious roads along which life took you, particularly the one that diverged in the yellow wood and into a clearing where your past became unexpectedly your present in ways you never could have anticipated.

He turned from the window and hobbled into his office. He eased himself into the chair in front of his laptop and shook his mouse. That caused the machine to issue sounds associated with someone old trying to climb a hill. His laptop was aging faster than he was.

When the machine finally calmed itself and began to operate properly, Tree clicked onto his e-mail and discovered, as usual, there was nothing of interest unless a "Payment Due" reminder from American Express could be deemed interesting. He sat staring at his screen. From the terrace came the sounds of laughter. That could only mean they were talking about him. Or was he being paranoid? Possibly, but then he reminded himself that paranoia was merely the state of being in possession of all the facts. More laughter from outside. They *were* talking about him.

Idly, he Googled Senator John Hardy. The senator's website homepage featured a tribute to his wife, Miranda: "I have lost my best friend and soulmate this past year. Miranda was everything to me. I don't know how to go on without her, but go on I must, because that's what she would have wanted."

There was no mention of the circumstances surrounding Miranda's death, and nothing about an affair with Chicago newscaster Kelly Fleming. Photographs of Miranda posted on the website showed a vibrant, attractive woman in her early fifties, hardly a candidate for suicide. But then what does a candidate for suicide look like? Like Miranda Hardy, apparently.

He found more photos taken at various campaign events with local Republican power brokers. Often the senator had his arm around his wife. The loving husband. Miranda posed with two young men identified as Senator Hardy's sons from another marriage. Finally, there was one photograph of Miranda looking proud as she embraced an unidentified young woman.

Glancing at the picture, Tree thought Miranda was with yet another loyal Republican at yet another fundraiser. He decided to close the page. He was tired, and this was getting him nowhere.

Then something struck him and he took another look at the young woman with Miranda Hardy. Were his tired eyes deceiving his aching head? He Googled Miranda's maiden name, but got nothing. The Internet regarded the senator's wife now and forever as Miranda Hardy.

He picked up the landline and dialed a number. It only rang twice before Tommy Dobbs said, "Mr. Callister? Is that you?"

"How are you doing, Tommy?"

"A whole lot better now that you've called. What's up?"

"Listen, Tommy, I know it's late but could you please make a phone call to the *Sun-Times* for me?"

"Sure, no problem. What is it you want to know?"

"I need to know Miranda Hardy's maiden name."

That created a silence on the other end of the phone. "Are you on to something, Mr. Callister?"

"I don't know yet, Tommy." When all else fails, Tree thought, try telling the truth.

"But if there is something, you'll share it with me, right?"

"At this moment, there's nothing to share. As soon as there is, believe me, you'll be the first to get it."

"All right, let me get back to you," he said and hung up.

Renewed laughter drifted up from the terrace. He could not be providing all that mirth, could he? He exhaled loudly. Yes, he concluded, he could.

The shrill ring of the landline made him jump. In this age of singing and vibrating smartphones, the sound of an actual telephone jangled the nerves.

When he picked up, Tommy Dobbs said, "I don't know what it's going to mean to you, Mr. Callister. But I've got that name for you."

———————

The streets of Cape Coral were all but deserted, the sodium-vapor streetlamps creating a surreal light that made it seem as though he were driving through an alternate world, a Mad Hatter's universe where everything was upside down and where, if you thought about it long enough, you could connect the most unlikely dots.

He told himself that he was not nuts, that the very act of leaving the house and easing behind the wheel of the Beetle was worth the searing pain, that it was necessary to practically cry out every time he took a breath. He had left the laughing Tree wives without saying anything. He wanted to do this, and did not want to hear a lot of questions accompanied by a chorus of objections. Better to do this now and worry about the objections later.

The mall with the red tile roof was dark, but the surrounding parking area was bathed in light. Brittany Pools in her bikini smiled at him from the side of her van. He was standing there in pain, thinking what a dumb idea this was when the driver's side door opened and Brittany got out.

She jerked in surprise when she saw him. She wore a scoop-necked top, a short white skirt, and an uncertain smile. "What are you doing here?" she said.

"I was hoping to find you," Tree said.

"What's this about?" Her voice was tense, guarded.

"Is there someplace we can talk?"

"Right here is fine," she said. "What is it you want to talk about?"

"Like I told you, I'm trying to help my friend, Rex."

"Yes, and I told you everything I know."

"I don't think you did, Brittany."

"That's not true," she answered.

"You didn't tell me you knew Kelly Fleming."

"I didn't know her," Brittany said.

"Your mother did."

When Brittany didn't say anything, Tree went on: "Your mother is Miranda Hardy. Her maiden name is Pools."

Brittany's voice grew tenser when she said, "I don't want to talk about this." As she spoke, she opened the flap of her purse.

"So then you did know Kelly?"

"I told you the truth. I never saw her at the house."

"But you knew about her."

"I knew there were all sorts of lies and rumors about my mother after she died. But that's all I knew. When I found out Kelly Fleming was with Mr. Baxter on the island, I actually went around to the chamber and gave him such a great deal on pool cleaning that he dropped the service he was using and hired me. I thought for sure I would see Kelly, and I wasn't sure how I would react when I did. But strangely enough, I never did see her—until I found her body."

"Did you tell the police who your mother was?"

She hesitated before she said, "The police know what they need to know."

"I also wanted to ask you about Alexei Markov," Tree said.

Her eyes widened and she stiffened even more. "What have you been doing? Are you following me?"

"Like I said, I'm trying to help Rex."

"Are you kidding?" she flared. "You're like this old pervert, running around stalking me. That's what's going on here."

"That's not the case," Tree said. "You're Miranda Hardy's daughter. You found the body of your mother's former lover. You're having an affair with Alexei Markov. That's not stalking you, Brittany, that's trying to understand what's going on here. Help me do that."

"There's nothing to understand," she said. "My mother's death has nothing to do with what happened here."

"Are you sure about that?"

"Mr. Markov employs me to clean his pool. That's all there is to it. Now leave me alone."

"I'm sorry, Brittany, but I think you're lying."

She reached inside her open purse. When her hand reappeared it was holding a small pistol. It looked like a toy gun. Only Tree didn't think it was a toy. She pointed it at him.

"That's not necessary," he said.

"Yeah, well, I think it is. A woman alone getting out of her vehicle late at night, accosted by a stranger. Who could blame her for protecting herself?"

"I'm just looking for some answers," Tree said. "I think you can give them to me."

"The answer, no matter what else you think, is that your friend Mr. Baxter killed that woman. If you think I had anything to do with it, you're nuts."

"Or maybe I'm not," Tree said.

"Get real about what happened and stop poking your nose into places where it doesn't belong. Places that could get you shot."

"I don't think shooting me would be that easy to explain," Tree said.

"Don't make me find out," she said. "Just back away and get out of here."

This wasn't getting him anywhere, he decided. Too many people with guns in South Florida, and they all seemed to be pointing at him. It was late. He was suddenly very tired. Connecting dots that didn't lead anywhere could do that to you.

26

By the time he arrived home, Tree's body parts were on fire. Inside, the Tree Wives Club had disbanded for the night. Only one member was still up. Freddie remained in place on the terrace, sipping at a glass of sparkling water.

With great pain, he bent to give her a kiss. She responded. More or less.

"You look terrible," she said.

"I feel terrible," he replied.

"You should have told me you were going out. I was worried."

"I know, but if I said anything, I'd have had three wives telling me not to go."

"Actually, only one wife would be saying anything. The other two don't count."

"But you see my point?"

"Not really, but tell me where you went."

He groaned into a chair opposite Freddie and told her what he had found out about Brittany Pools.

"So what do you think?" Freddie said when he finished. "You think Brittany killed Kelly because she believed Kelly is responsible for her mother's suicide?"

"She denies it, of course. But you've got to admit it's a possibility. If you're looking for motive, there it is."

"Still, you can equally argue that Kelly was having an affair with Miranda Hardy and Rex found out about it. When Kelly decided not to marry him, he lost control and in a jealous rage accidentally killed her."

"The point is, there is now another possibility, something that could make a jury think twice about convicting Rex."

"Do you really think this Brittany Pools is sleeping with Alexei? And if she is, how does that fit in?"

"Judy thinks she is. And Brittany certainly didn't like it when I asked her about Alexei. If she is his mistress, I'm not sure it isn't just a wild coincidence that has nothing to do with Kelly Fleming's murder. Or maybe it does and so far I can't make the connection."

"I'm afraid we're not going to solve this tonight," Freddie said.

"I wish I could shake off the feeling that I'm the wrong guy for this. I'm not a real detective."

"Then what are you?"

"The word fraud comes to mind."

"Don't be so hard on yourself," Freddie said. "I don't like the way you did it, but I think you made progress tonight. At least now there is another possible suspect other than Rex, and you certainly didn't have that before."

"I hope you're right."

"Come along, my aging and sore detective hero, it's time for bed."

"Are the other two members of the Tree Wives Club bedded down?"

"Tree Wives Club?" Freddie said. "Yes, I suppose we are, aren't we? I tucked the other two members, filled with wine, into their beds about an hour ago."

"Kind of weird, the way things are turning out."

"We are a curious club, no question. A very restricted membership. But I like Judy and Skye, and they certainly need help right now."

"But?"

"I suppose I find it hard to believe you were married to either woman, if you want me to be honest."

"It can't have happened, there must be some mistake," Tree said. "I have to pinch myself to be reminded that I once had another life entirely."

"Other lives," Freddie reminded.

"It's all a blur, so far back in my murky past. Yet here they are, these two women I barely recognize, both claiming they were married to me."

Freddie rose from her chair, yawned, and stretched. "I've had too much wine and listened to far too many tall tales about a certain husband."

"Don't tell me," Tree said with a groan.

"Don't worry, my lips are sealed." She bent to him. "Except when it comes to kissing you."

"For that I am forever grateful," Tree said.

"You should be." Her lips pressed against his. He stood up and held her against him.

Held her for a long time—until the doorbell rang.

27

Freddie opened the door to find Sanibel Police detective Owen Markfield on the threshold. As Tree usually did when he saw Markfield, he groaned. As Markfield usually did when he saw Tree, he cast a malevolent glare.

"This late?" Tree said.

"Let's talk outside, Tree," Markfield said in the authoritative voice that drove Tree crazy.

"Are you alone?"

"Detective Boone isn't available."

"I'm not so sure we should be alone together," Tree said.

That inspired a rare Markfield smile. "I promise not to hurt you, Tree. Let's go outside."

He followed Markfield out the door and down the stairs to where Markfield had parked his unmarked sedan. Markfield noticed the way he was walking—or hobbling. "Something wrong with you?"

"Couple of broken ribs, that's all," Tree said.

"You live on the edge," Markfield said dryly.

"Not me," Tree said. "I'm just an older retired guy."

"Let's talk inside my car," Markfield said. He opened the passenger door for Tree and then went around to the driver's side and got in.

Pine scent filled the car. To hide the smell of fear the vehicle's occupants gave off? Tree wondered. Markfield occupied himself flipping through the pages of the notebook he always produced when Tree was around. Turning pages full of confessions, Tree imagined, trying to find space to record another one. But confess to what?"

"What's this about?" Tree said. His voice sounded shaky in the dimness of the car.

"Give me a moment here," Markfield said. He reached inside his jacket and found a pen. "Can you tell me where you were earlier this evening, Tree?"

"I was home," Tree said.

"That's all?"

"You still haven't told me what this is about," Tree countered.

"Right now, it's about you telling me where you were tonight," Markfield said.

"I had to go out earlier," Tree said.

"Yeah? Where did you go?"

"I went to see someone in Cape Coral in connection with a case."

"What case was that, Tree?"

"Come on, Markfield. You know what case I'm talking about."

"Who did you see in Cape Coral?"

"What difference does that make?"

"Just answer the question."

"The woman's name is Brittany Pools."

"What time was this? What time did you visit her?"

"It was about nine o'clock."

"Nine o'clock this evening?"

"That's right."

Markfield fell silent while he scribbled into his notebook. Tree never liked it when he was doing that. Markfield scribbling was usually a sign of bad things to come.

Markfield looked up from his notebook. "How long were you with Brittany Pools?"

"I don't know. Not long. She didn't want to talk to me, so I left."

"And she was all right when you left?"

"She was fine." Now Tree was really worried. "Markfield, what's going on here? What's happened?"

Markfield stopped writing in his notebook and gave Tree a hard look, intimidating in the darkness. Tree should have been used to those looks by now, but they still unnerved him.

"I got a call about an hour ago from the Cape Coral police. They're investigating the death of Brittany Pools."

"What happened?" The words caught in Tree's throat.

"According to my friends at Cape Coral homicide, her body was found in her van about ten p.m.

"Who found her?"

"I have no idea."

"What was the cause of death?"

"Blunt force trauma is the way it's described."

"You mean someone beat her to death."

"That's what it sounds like, yeah."

"I'm in shock," Tree said.

"Are you?"

"What's that supposed to mean?"

"I don't know. The Cape Coral detectives apparently picked you up on a video monitor mounted at the mall where the body was found. That's how they got the license number of your car. The two of you appeared to be arguing. According to detectives, she actually pulled a gun on you at one point. Is that true?"

"It is, but that would seem to be evidence that I didn't kill her, not that I did."

"I don't know about that," Markfield said.

"If they have videos of the two of us together, they must be able to see that I left, and they must have some record of what happened after I was gone."

"I have no idea what they have or haven't got," Markfield said. "Obviously, the investigation is still in its formative stages. I got a phone call from a friend of mine over at Cape Coral asking me to help them out and have a talk with you."

"Which you are only too happy to do," Tree said.

"I am happy to do anything that might result in you going to prison," Markfield said.

"Sorry to disappoint you, but this isn't going to do it."

"Don't be so sure about that," Markfield said. He put his notebook aside and reached forward and turned the key in the ignition. The motor started up.

"What are you doing?" Tree demanded.

"I'm taking you in for further questioning."

"It's two o'clock in the morning. Don't do this."

"You're not resisting arrest are you, Callister?"

Even in the darkness, Tree could see the hopeful glint in Markfield's eye. He asked, "Am I under arrest?"

"You could be."

Headlights flooded the interior of the car as a Lexus pulled into the drive and parked beside them. Tree turned to see the welcome form of T. Emmett Hawkins ease out of the Lexus. Hawkins in an open-necked shirt without his trademark bow tie, rapped on Markfield's window.

Markfield scowled before flicking at the tab that electronically lowered the window.

Hawkins said, "Good morning, Detective."

Markfield bobbed his head slightly but didn't say anything. Tree took the opportunity to get out of the car. Hawkins turned to Tree as he came around the rear. "And good morning to you, Tree."

"Emmett," Tree said. "This is a pleasant surprise."

"I specialize in them," Hawkins said. He returned his attention to Markfield. "I assume you are finished with my client, Detective."

"He wants me to come to the station with him," Tree said.

"Why would you want him to do that, Detective?"

"I have more questions for him," Markfield said in a sullen voice.

"I'm sorry, sir, but unless you have reason to hold my client, he's not going anywhere."

Markfield kept his focus trained straight ahead.

"Do you have any reason to hold him?"

"We'll continue this another time," Markfield said.

"The next time you want to talk to my client, please make sure I am present, Detective."

Markfield pressed the tab that started the driver's side window up. The lawyer said, "Good morning to you, sir."

Markfield backed out onto the roadway, and then sped away along Andy Rosse Lane.

Freddie came down the steps as Hawkins turned to Tree. "What am I to do with you, Tree? You really must stop going off with police officers searching for any excuse to put you behind bars."

Freddie reached Tree and said, "Are you all right?"

"Thanks to Emmett here, I'm not spending the rest of the night in jail."

"Thank your wife for once again coming to your rescue and promptly calling me," Hawkins said. "Now please tell me what Detective Markfield was doing here."

"Earlier this evening, I found out that Brittany Pools is the daughter of Miranda Hardy, the Chicago senator's wife who committed suicide after Kelly broke off their affair."

"So you confronted this woman?"

"I drove out to Cape Coral to talk to Brittany. She admitted she was Miranda's daughter, but when I tried to question her further, she pulled a gun and told me to leave."

"Which I presume you did."

"Yes."

"And after you left?"

"According to what Markfield just told me, someone bludgeoned Brittany to death."

Hawkins frowned. "That's unfortunate on a number of levels. Not the least of which, it makes it more difficult to present Brittany as a possible suspect in Kelly Fleming's murder."

"That doesn't mean she didn't kill Kelly. She certainly had the motive."

"Blaming Kelly for her mother's death," Hawkins said. "Yes, we could certainly have thrown a wrench into the machinery of the state's case with that revelation."

"Couldn't it still?" Tree said. "I hate to say it, but Brittany's murder doesn't make it less likely that she killed Kelly."

"Juries tend to take a skeptical view of using dead people as possible murder suspects," Hawkins said. "But we will see. In the meantime, I will remind you again, Tree, do not speak to the police unless I am with you."

Yes, right, Tree thought. Otherwise, before I know it, the police could be arresting me for murder.

28

Pat, pumped full of wine, had slept right through Tree's encounter with Detective Owen Markfield, but Judy was wide awake and upset when Tree told her and Freddie over an early morning cup of coffee that Brittany Pools was dead.

Markfield, focused on Tree as a possible suspect in her murder, was probably a long way from connecting Brittany to Alexei Markov. But Judy wasn't far at all.

"What do you think, Judy?" Tree asked.

"There is no end to the things Alexei is capable of, I suppose, and I am scared of him, but why would he kill her?"

"And the answer is?" Freddie chimed in.

Judy thought for a moment before she said, "I don't know. I just don't know."

Freddie said, "The generic answer usually is something like, because he wanted to keep her quiet."

"Yes, Alexei doesn't want anyone talking too loudly about his affairs," Judy agreed.

That was the cue for Pat to appear. Tree expected her to look bleary-eyed and hungover, but she was bright and alert, skin aglow. That was it with Pat, he now remembered. She could party hearty with the best of the newsroom wild men and still be at work first thing the next morning as though nothing had happened. Meanwhile, everyone else could barely lift their heads up as they reached for coffee and aspirin.

Freddie poured her coffee while Pat expressed disbelief at having slept through the police at two in the morning. It then was necessary to tell her what had happened. She took it all in, making sympathetic noises. But she seem distracted as, Tree recalled, Pat always was during their marriage when she wasn't particularly interested in the topic under discussion—in this case the murder of someone she didn't know and could not care less about.

It soon became apparent that she had something else on her mind. It was not long before it came out. "I got a call from Tal Fiala a few minutes ago," she said.

"The boyfriend you're supposedly running away from," Tree said.

Pat frowned, not liking that description. "He's not my *boyfriend.*" She paused. "Well, I suppose in one sense he *was* my boyfriend. But he's not anymore."

"I stand corrected," Tree said.

"Anyway, Tal wants to see me."

Freddie said, "Do you want to see him, Skye?"

"I don't know. I guess I should see what he wants. But I don't want to meet him alone, that's for sure." She looked at Tree. "Would you come with me?"

The last thing he needed first thing this morning. He was tired, and it still seemed like every inch of his body was hurting. All he wanted to do was go back to bed.

"I'm not so sure you should be anywhere near this man," Freddie said to Pat.

"I would do it if Tree goes with me," Pat said.

"Where does Tal want to meet?"

"In Palm Beach," she said.

"You want to drive over there?" Tree tried to keep the exhaustion out of his voice, but didn't do a very good job of it.

"I don't want him coming here," Pat said. "He doesn't know where I am, and I'd just as soon keep it that way."

Freddie addressed Tree: "What do you think?"

"He won't do anything if you're there," Pat interjected. "We drive over, hear what he has to say and then get out of there."

"And you have no idea what he wants?"

"Tree?" Freddie gave Tree that look that always indicated he should cooperate. He sighed and said, "Let me take a shower and get cleaned up."

"You're a sweetheart," Pat said. She kissed him fiercely on the lips.

"Well," Judy said, her eyes widening. "That's interesting."

———————

Pat said she didn't want to make a fuss, and then as Pat tended to do, proceeded to make a fuss. She simply could not return to Palm Beach in the Chevy Spark she had been driving or in Tree's beaten up old rattletrap of a Volkswagen. The thought brought a flood of tears. Freddie was consoling. Freddie agreed to provide her Mercedes, allowing Pat to return to Palm Beach in the style to which she had become accustomed.

She had dressed for her meeting with Tal Fiala, a black knee-length pencil skirt accompanied by a plain white top of silken material and a pale-green linen jacket. The makeup had been carefully applied. Tal would receive full-force Pat today

"Freddie really is a dream," Pat said, like a cat unfolding sensuously on the passenger seat. "You are a lucky man, you know that, don't you, Tree? To have finally found someone who supports you without question, doesn't mind that you don't have a cent to your name, and who is also willing to overlook your shortcomings."

"My shortcomings," Tree said, keeping his eyes on the road, fighting the urge to wring his ex-wife's neck.

"Hey, we all have them," she said. And then she grinned: "Even me."

"Not you, Pat," Tree said through gritted teeth.

"I've done a lot of work with myself the past couple of years, trying to understand the *me* in me, realizing I've had to change certain things in my life."

Tree felt he had no choice but to ask, "What sorts of things?"

"That creep Tal Fiala for starters."

"Did you decide this before or after the two of you were indicted and he threatened to kill you?"

Pat's sunny mood evaporated. "He didn't threaten to *kill* me per se. I may have exaggerated that a little bit."

"You exaggerated? Or you lied?"

"Look, I don't know what Tal is capable of, but I was worried. I thought it best to get out of town for a while. Give myself some distance. Elevation."

"So Tal hasn't threatened you?"

"You think I'm guilty, don't you, Tree? That's at the bottom of these constant insinuations, isn't it?"

"I'm not insinuating anything. I'm wondering what you're up to."

"For your information, Tree, I am innocent until I am proven guilty," she stated in a shaky voice. "And I will not be proven guilty, I can tell you that right now. And incidentally, I would remind you that I am now called Skye. You just refuse to deal with that fact. You always were bull-headed and difficult, you know that, don't you? I'm not sure how Freddie puts up with you, I'm really not."

The tears returned as they usually did when Pat felt pushed into a corner, threatened with actually having to confront the truth of her actions.

Tree said, "Okay, Skye. Sorry, I didn't mean to upset you."

"I'm not upset." She produced a tissue and blew her nose into it. "I'm past getting upset about these things. I'm strong. I really am."

"Yes, you are," Tree agreed.

"People will know soon enough that I'm not guilty. That's why it was imperative that I don't come back to town in that awful car of yours. That's why it was so generous of Freddie to lend us her car."

"What do you think?" Tree said. "People will believe you're innocent if they see you in a Mercedes?"

"It certainly won't hurt," Pat said, brushing at her tears.

"Thankfully, you're in the right car, so how do we handle this once we get to town?"

She was about to blow her nose for a third time. The question stopped her. "What do you mean?"

"When we meet Tal. How do you want to handle it?"

"Oh, gosh, Tree, these questions. I don't know. Let's just get there and worry about it then."

"You think that's a good idea? Don't you think we should have some sort of game plan?"

"I can't think right now, Tree. I'm too tense. We'll deal with it as soon as we get to Palm Beach. I'm a very sensitive person. I don't react well to pressure. You know that about me, don't you? I've grown so much since we were married. We just have to get through this and then everything will be all right again. You can see that, can't you?"

Tree didn't say anything.

29

The rich hid in the fortress-mansions along South Ocean Drive behind lush hedges and low walls. The rich were very quiet, Tree thought as he drove along the drive. They remained in their ocean-view fortresses and spoke in hushed tones so as not to rouse the rabble.

Pat, acknowledging her ties to the silent rich, had also grown quiet. Uncharacteristically so. Tense and fidgety.

She shifted and played with her hair, lost in thought.

"Everything all right?" Tree asked.

"It's just a little farther along here," she said.

"What's along here?"

"Tal's place. Where I want you to stop."

"That game plan we talked about."

"Let's not worry about that," Pat said.

"I still want to know what happens when we get there. Is Tal going to meet us?"

"It'll be okay," she said vaguely. "It's just ahead."

A couple of minutes later, she directed him to turn right through a break in perfectly squared hedges. Sand-colored pillars flanked a tiled drive running to a Spanish-style house. Four towering palms in front of the house suffered from that most common of local afflictions, anorexia.

Tree brought the Mercedes to a stop. Pat had gone pale. She played some more with her hair and said, "That's fine."

"What's fine?"

"I want you to wait here," she said.

"Where are you going?"

"Where do you think I'm going?" she answered irritably. "I'm going inside."

"I thought you wanted me with you."

"Let me check to make sure everything's okay, and then I'll come back for you."

"Are you sure about this?"

"Please, Tree. Don't argue."

Pat opened the passenger door and slid out. He watched her cross the drive to the solid oak front door recessed into the façade of the house. The door opened—or did Pat open it?—and she disappeared inside.

Tree sat with the window down listening to the insects that enliven a languid summer afternoon in Florida. Occasionally, the sound of a car swishing past on South Ocean Drive crept over the hedges, and the breeze brought the wash of waves on the nearby shore. The rich, whatever they were doing at this hour, continued to do it quietly.

Given the silence and the heat, Tree did what he usually did on these occasions, he began to fall asleep. He told himself he was not going to do that. He would remain alert in case Pat needed him. After all, that's what he was here for, wasn't he? He began to wonder.

Despite his best efforts, he must have drifted off because the next thing he was jerking awake with no idea how long he had been out. There was no sign of Pat. He shook himself awake, feeling cramped inside the Mercedes. He opened the door and eased himself out. His busted rib cage cried objection. He grimaced and leaned against the car before straightening himself and staring at the mansion. It appeared empty although around here the whole world seemed to be deserted, as though such sunny perfection should not be marred by human presence.

He looked at his watch. Pat had been gone for three quarters of an hour. She should have come back by now. Shouldn't she? He walked over to the entrance, debating what to do.

Finally, he entered the alcove framing the massive oak door. He tried the latch. It stuck a bit, but the door opened. He pushed it open further and stepped inside.

A high-ceilinged ivory foyer was overhung with an ornate light fixture borrowed from Louis XIV. The sound of his footsteps echoed on the marble floor. He stifled the urge to call Pat's name—he should holler for Skye—moving from the foyer into an equally white great room with a coffered ceiling and a fireplace. Floor-to-ceiling French doors gave a view of a lawn you could putt on. There wasn't a speck of dust anywhere. Nothing was a centimeter out of place.

This was immaculate, undiscovered country, and he was its first explorer. He must be very careful not to muss up anything—and certainly stay away from the canvas mounted on an easel beside the fireplace. It was the oil acquired at the Palm Beach Jewelry, Art, and Antique Show, the two-fisted guy in a fedora with the half-naked blonde, James Alfred Meese's work given a place of honor in Tal's house.

He was studying the painting, wondering what Tal saw in it beyond a certain attractive pulpy luridness when the first gunshot broke the luxurious silence.

The sound of a second shot caused him reflexively to duck down. Tal Fiala veered into view with what looked like a Glock automatic pistol in his hand. He saw Tree and stopped in his tracks. "What the hell are you doing here?"

"I came with Pat," Tree said.

"You've betrayed me," he cried. "You've both betrayed me!"

"What are you talking about?" Tree demanded. "Where's Pat?"

"Tal, please, come back here." Pat's panicky voice descending from somewhere upstairs.

"Move!" he said to Tree.

"Move where?" Tree demanded.

"Tal, please!" Pat sounded even more desperate.

Tal pushed Tree out of the way so he could grab the Meese painting off the easel. The painting in one hand, the gun in the other, he swung around to Tree.

"Get out," Tal said. "Get out the door or so help me God I will shoot you."

Tree reeled back, shoved by the panicky, gun-wielding Tal out of the great room into the foyer. Tree fumbled with the door, Tal holding the painting, screaming something unintelligible in his ear. The door opened and Tree stumbled out.

Caught in a blur of sunlight, squinting into the brightness, Tree realized the drive around the entrance was no longer deserted, but filling with grim-faced men and women in blue windbreakers and baseball caps, all with outstretched arms ending in hands clasped around guns. The guns, Tree noticed, were pointed at him. The gun-toting, baseball cap-wearing men and women were shouting at the top of their lungs. Dimly, Tree was aware that they seemed to be ordering him to get down on the ground. They also wanted him to drop the gun. Were they demented? He didn't have a gun.

He tripped over one of the paving stones and went sprawling forward. That's when the world exploded around him. He hit the ground, scrapping his hands, twisting around in time to see Tal doing a curious dance, his multicolored shirt blowing like a sail in a strong wind, holding the Meese painting up like a shield. The canvas was punctured by holes, and the dance wasn't so much a dance as it was the death throes of an armed man hit by a hail of bullets.

Tal dropped the painting and collapsed to the pavement close to Tree. Tal's eyes were wide open, but they were no longer seeing anything.

For endless minutes the world was silent again and nothing moved in it. Then the silence was punctuated with screams as Pat flew out the door, rushing to the fallen Tal. Crying hysterically, she threw herself on top of him. That lasted only a few seconds before the men and women with the guns came to their senses and started shouting things Tree still couldn't understand. Why did everyone yell unintelligibly in these circumstances? Tree wondered. The frantic Pat was lifted away from the body of her dead lover—the lover whose death, Tree suspected, his former wife was more than a little responsible for.

"Mr. Callister?" a voice said. Tree looked up to see a familiar face taking shape against the sunlight. "Mr. Callister, what the hell are you doing here?"

Tree gazed at the canvas on the ground. There was now a bullet hole where the two-fisted guy's head had been.

What was he doing here? A darned good question, Tree thought.

30

Special FBI Agent Shawn Lazenby removed his baseball cap and sat down beside Tree in the immaculate ivory salon. Tree was slumped back on one of the white sofas facing the white fireplace. Sitting like this eased the pain in his ribs. A medic had smeared his scrapped palms with Neosporin. In addition to his aching sides, Tree could add burning hands to his growing list of maladies.

Through the French doors lots of men and women in blue windbreakers emblazoned with the initials FBI were visible, milling around with uniformed Palm Beach police officers. Most of the law-enforcement population of South Florida appeared to have turned up for the post-shooting ceremonies. What did they all do, Tree wondered, beyond standing around, looking important as they spoke in low voices to one another?

Inside this white room, however, all was quiet except for the calm voice of Special Agent Lazenby saying, "Mr. Callister you sure do turn up in the strangest places."

Lazenby's youthful Asian face, artfully-spiked black hair, and calm professional manner belied the hothead Tree had encountered years ago. Or maybe it was simply that time and experience had mellowed him.

"You're looking good, Agent Lazenby," Tree said.

"I guess married life agrees with me, Mr. Callister. We have two kids now. A boy and a girl."

"That's great," Tree said. "Your wife's with the FBI, too?"

Lazenby grinned and shook his head. "No way. She's a schoolteacher. The bad guys in her life get detentions."

"No shootouts in Florida mansions."

Lazenby's face became solemn. "That was unfortunate," he said. "It wasn't supposed to go down that way."

"It's what happens when everyone's got a gun," Tree said.

Lazenby studied him for a couple of beats and then said, "I've just got a few questions for you."

"Sure," Tree said. "But what about Pat?"

"If you mean Skye, she's shaken up as you can imagine. We've taken her to the hospital for observation."

"But she's all right?"

"She's going to be fine. Like I say, things weren't supposed to unfold the way they did—and we're certainly not pleased that she got you mixed up in this. We knew nothing about it. I'm not sure what she was thinking."

"What exactly did she get me mixed up in?"

"Miss Laine had agreed to help us with our investigation into the activities of Tal Fiala." Lazenby had adopted his formal FBI agent voice. "She was meeting with him today in order to extract information that could prove useful in our investigation."

"In return for a reduced sentence," Tree said.

"Something like that, yes."

"In other words, when she arrived for the meeting today, she was wearing a wire."

"In the course of their encounter, Mr. Fiala apparently got wind of what was going on and that's when the situation deteriorated. We thought Ms. Laine was in imminent danger and we decided to move in."

"Guns blazing."

"Unfortunately, Mr. Fiala decided to go that route. Nobody was more surprised than we were. He just didn't seem the type to engage in a shootout with federal officers."

"Now he's dead."

"And you are lucky to be alive if I may say so, Mr. Callister. How did you get mixed up with Ms. Laine in the first place?"

"I used to be married to her."

"You're kidding."

"It was a long time ago in Chicago. But when she got in trouble with the law here, she called me, thinking I was still in the private investigation business."

"But you're not?"

"I'm supposed to be retired."

"Some retirement," Lazenby said.

"I'm surprised that the FBI is involved in this."

"What is it you think we're involved in, Mr. Callister?"

"As I understand it, Tal used Pat to defraud a local woman suffering from Alzheimer's by siphoning money out of her account."

"Yes, all that is more or less true, although I think Ms. Laine in talking to you has somewhat diminished the role she played."

"This doesn't sound like the sort of federal case that would involve you and all these agents."

"I probably shouldn't be telling you all this," Lazenby said. "But now that you're involved, I suppose you should be aware of the wider picture."

"There is a wider picture?"

Lazenby nodded. "The reason Tal Fiala was defrauding the Alzheimer's patient, we believe, was because he was desperate for money. Thanks to Ms. Laine, he found a quick way to obtain it."

Tree glanced around him. "He lived here and he was desperate for money?"

"Fiala was involved in a money-laundering scheme, taking money from people not nearly as innocent as a little old lady suffering dementia—and a whole lot less willing to put up with being ripped off."

"He was ripping people off?"

"Tal liked to gamble. He was using other people's money to indulge his passion. They didn't like that."

"Who? Who didn't like it?"

"Most notably, a wealthy Russian residing in Florida. One of those oligarchs you hear about. The intention today with Ms. Laine was not so much to gather evidence as it was to force Mr. Fiala to cooperate in netting a much bigger fish."

"The Russian."

"With Fiala dead, I'm afraid we are back to square one."

"How much did Pat know about the money laundering?"

"You know Ms. Laine now prefers to be called Skye?"

"Yes, she's growing. Evolving."

"I'm afraid she still has more work to do," Lazenby said dryly.

"How much did she know?"

Lazenby allowed another smile. "Ms. Laine, as I'm sure you understand, has many admirable qualities. Unfortunately, judgment when it comes to men does not appear to be one of those qualities."

"Our marriage was a testament to that," Tree said.

"She is a very naïve woman. We are straining to give her the benefit of the doubt over the fraud thing. However, we do not believe she was involved in Mr. Fiala's other activities and knew nothing about them until we came along."

"What's going to happen to her now?"

"We'll have to see," Lazenby said. "On the one hand, she delivered on her end of our arrangement. On the other hand, we don't have Tal Fiala. I'm not sure how the Palm Beach district attorney is going to feel about letting her off the hook."

"What about this Russian guy?"

"Like I said, we are more or less back to square one. We know who he is, we know what he's up to, but without Fiala we don't have enough to bring charges against him."

"Who is this guy?"

Lazenby said, "I'm afraid I'm not at liberty to tell you that."

That was all right, Tree thought. He knew of one rich Russian in South Florida who would do nicely.

A police officer stood guard outside Pat's room at the Palm Beach Hospital. Special Agent Lazenby had phoned ahead, and the officer allowed Tree inside. Pat came awake as he seated himself beside her. She looked so pale and small and lost in the hospital bed that Tree couldn't bring himself to be mad at her.

"Tree," she whispered in a slurry voice. "Boy, am I glad to see you."

"How are you doing?" he asked, taking her hand.

"I'm okay, just tired." Tears were in her eyes. Her hand tightened in his. "Oh, Tree, you didn't get shot or anything?"

"I was able to duck in time," Tree said.

"I tried to tell those FBI creeps that he was crazy, but all they saw was this smooth-talking a-hole. Well, now they know, don't they?"

"The important thing is, you're not hurt."

"Tal was so crazy, Tree. Really, he was. That's why he thought he could shoot it out with half the FBI agents in Florida."

"They should have listened to you, no question, and avoided all this."

"I shouldn't have lied to you," she said.

"You didn't lie to me," Tree said. He smiled at her. "You just withheld certain information, that's all."

"I just couldn't go there alone," she said. "I just couldn't. So I guess I tricked you into coming with me, and I'm sorry about that. I nearly got you killed."

"Don't worry, they can't kill me," Tree said, very much aware that they could.

"But Tal is dead, Tree, and it's all my fault." More tears.

Tree held her hand tighter. "You had nothing to do with Tal deciding to pull a gun."

"As much of a lunatic as he was," Pat said between hiccupping sobs.

"I never expected him to do something like that."

"Did they tell you what Tal was doing?"

"They said he was involved in some sort of money-laundering, and they kept at me to make him help them with a sting operation they were planning."

"Did they say who he was working with?"

She shook her head. "No, nothing like that. Just that they weren't after Tal so much as the people he was working for.

"We were talking, and I was trying to tell him that it would be better for both of us if we cooperated with law enforcement. As soon as I said that, he got this really suspicious look in his eyes. Tree, it was like he had a sixth sense or something that I was lying. All of a sudden he was on his feet, accusing me of betraying him. Then he tore at my blouse and he saw this... what the FBI had given me, and that's when he really, really lost it. I don't know where the gun came from but he had it in his hand, and he was running out of the room. I begged him not to do it, to stay with me. But he wasn't listening, and that's the last..."

The rest of what she said was lost amid a cacophony of hiccups and sobs. Tree didn't know what to do or say. He squeezed her hand and said, "It's going to be all right, Pat," when he knew it probably wasn't.

"What's going to happen to me, Tree?" Her eyes swirled with panic. "Do you suppose they're going to send me to jail?"

"The FBI says you did your part. If they made a deal with you, they should live up to it. Do you have a lawyer?"

She tried to smile through the tears. "I had one until a few hours ago."

"Is there anyone you can call?"

"I don't know," she said. "I don't know anything right now."

"I'll see what I can do," Tree said. He gently removed his hand from hers. "I'd better get back to Fort Myers. Freddie is going to be worried."

"Tell her I'm sorry, Tree. Tell her I screwed up everything and I am so sorry."

"She likes you, Skye. She'll be relieved you're okay."

Pat's smile brightened. "You called me Skye," she said.

31

Freddie had already heard a version of events in Palm Beach on the radio so that when Tree got home she hugged him as soon as he was in the door, mumbling into his chest something like, "Thank goodness you're all right."

"For once no one shot me," Tree said, holding her.

"How do you always manage to get yourself mixed up in this stuff?"

"I asked myself that same question many times on the drive back," Tree said. "The more I say I'm out of the private detective business, the more I seem to be in it, complete with a lot of people shooting guns."

"What about Skye? How's she?"

"They've got her in hospital overnight for observation. After that, I'm not sure what's going to happen. It turns out the FBI had made a deal with her to be part of a sting operation designed to trap Tal Fiala who wasn't just ripping off old ladies. He was also laundering money for the Russians."

"You're kidding," Freddie said.

"Somehow Tal discovered Skye was wearing a wire. When he tried to escape, that's when the FBI closed in and the shooting started."

"And she dragged you into all this and never said a thing?"

"She's very sorry," Tree said.

"It's a little late for sorry. I can't imagine what she was thinking."

"Now that we're on the subject of ex-wives," Tree said, "where's Judy?"

"Not to complicate your life any more than it already is…"

"No, don't tell me," said Tree in a voice more anguished than he expected.

"Alexei's in intensive care. They think he suffered a heart attack. Judy went off to be with him."

"She went off to be with Alexei? The guy she's afraid might kill her if she goes back to Moscow?"

"I tried to point that out to her, but she decided to play the dutiful wife."

"She should stay as far away from him as she can," Tree said.

Freddie caught the undercurrent in his voice. "That sounds as though you know something you should be telling me."

"I'm not entirely certain of this, but you remember my old friend Shawn Lazenby?"

"The FBI agent from Miami?"

Tree nodded. "According to Agent Lazenby, Tal Fiala was laundering money for a Russian oligarch living in South Florida. The whole idea behind that sting operation was to get Tal to work with the bureau in order to build a case against this guy."

"And you think it's Alexei Markov?"

"How many other oligarchs are living around here?"

"I don't know," Freddie said. "Did Lazenby tell you it was Markov?"

"He didn't," Tree had to admit.

Freddie said, "For all we know, there could be flocks of oligarchs in Florida."

"I'm putting my money on Markov."

"For now he's in the hospital and no threat to anyone," Freddie said.

"Let's hope so," Tree said.

———

Freddie grilled a couple of pieces of grouper, made a salad and added some rice for Tree. They ate out on the terrace as the day faded and the cries of the tourists rose again from the Mucky Duck.

By the time they finished, it was almost dark and Tree could hardly keep his eyes open. Freddie urged him to go to bed. "You're dead tired," she said.

"If I go to bed now, I'll be up in the middle of the night."

"No you won't. You'll be dreaming of Elizabeth Taylor."

He looked at her in astonishment. "How do you know?"

"Face it, my darling. I know everything about you—too much, probably."

"Seriously, how did you know?"

"You call out her name in your sleep."

"I do not," he said.

"Marilyn Monroe, too," Freddie said. "What do you do with them, anyway?"

"In my dreams?"

"Presumably, that's the only place you can do anything."

"They give me advice."

"What kind of advice?"

"About relationships and marriage, I think," Tree said. "It all seemed very insightful at the time, but then in the morning I can't remember a thing."

"You don't sleep with them?"

"I resist temptation," Tree said.

Freddie gave him a look suggesting total disbelief.

"I do," he insisted. "I tell them I'm all grown up now and don't need adolescent fantasies."

"As you dream adolescent fantasies."

"They are dreams of resistance," Tree insisted.

Instead of following Freddie to bed, Tree opted for a couple of old *Luther* episodes on Netflix. He loved the way Idris Elba as Detective Superintendent John Luther trampled through London, big, tough, and resilient, tracking down the city's latest malevolent serial killer in the span of an hour. He longed to be like John Luther—or he longed until he fell asleep.

The last thing he remembered, Luther had doused himself with gasoline and fired up his lighter all in pursuit of bringing the killer to justice. What a guy, Tree thought.

He jerked awake when Freddie reappeared in her pajamas, holding her cellphone.

"Judy wants to speak to you," Freddie said.

"Judy?"

"Your ex-wife. One of your ex-wives. Should I tell her you'll call her back?"

"No, I'll talk to her," Tree said. He got painfully to his feet and took tentative steps, gritting his teeth.

"Tree, you are not well," Freddie said worriedly.

"Takes me a moment to get going, that's all."

Tree took the phone from her.

Judy said, "Tree?"

"Yes, Judy. Are you all right?"

"I need to see you," she said.

"When?"

"As soon as possible," she replied.

"But you're all right?" he repeated. "We've been worried about you."

"Nothing to worry about, everything's under control, and I'm fine. I just need to see you. Do you suppose you could come out to the house?"

"Right now?"

"I wouldn't ask if it wasn't important."

32

The electronic gates on Coconut Drive had been repaired and this time were open to allow Tree to drive the Beetle straight through into the forecourt of a two-story white house fit for a Russian oligarch on Sanibel Island. A swimming pool the size of a landing strip shone through the darkness.

Tree parked the Beetle and got out as Valentin came out, circling around the pool. He was wearing his usual dark suit, but tonight he displayed something Tree had not seen before—a smile.

"Welcome, Mr. Callister." Jolly Valentin greeted him in a booming voice.

He held out his hand to Tree. Tree looked at it. "You've got to be kidding," he said.

The smile remained in place, but the hand didn't. "Mrs. Markov is waiting for you inside," Valentin said.

He turned and Tree followed him into a foyer nearly as impressive as Tal Fiala's in Palm Beach, with the added benefit that he didn't have to dodge bullets—at least not yet.

Valentin guided him into a sitting room that opened onto a light-bathed dock jutting into Roosevelt Channel. In daylight, he imagined the view encompassed the narrow headland that was Buck Key.

Judy was posed gazing out at the dock and the blackness beyond, as though waiting for her long-lost lover to return. Maybe she was, Tree mused. Maybe he was the long lost lover.

"Mr. Callister to see you," announced Valentin.

Judy turned to give Tree the sort of professional smile reserved for former husbands, not long-lost lovers. "Thank you, Valentin," she said.

And Valentin, the thug transformed into the good servant, disappeared.

"There you are, Tree," she said in that lilting tone he had heard many times when arriving home from Chicago booze cans far too late at night.

Judy appeared surprisingly calm and cool considering what she had recently been through with the evil Alexei Markov. She wore white slacks that did not distract from the multi-colored blouse or the chunky necklace at her throat. Her hair was perfection, makeup impeccable. Tree wondered if a new Judy hadn't been sent over from a boutique that specialized in producing more elegant versions of one's wife.

"Well, you certainly look all right," Tree said.

"I've never been better, Tree. Thanks for coming at such short notice. Would you like something? Some sparkling water?"

"No, thanks, Judy."

She glided over to one of the two sofas strategically placed on either side of a fireplace that reminded him of the one in Palm Beach. The cold-hearted criminal rich apparently needed to warm themselves by a fireplace even if Florida and fireplaces didn't exactly go together. Tree sat so that he faced her, feeling curiously on edge, as if he had been summoned by his high school principal. Or perhaps it was Judy's newly-minted self-confidence previously hidden from him and everyone else.

"Tree, I must tell you that Alexei is still in the hospital and, frankly, it does not look good." Judy said.

"What's happened to him?" Tree asked.

"Alexei has suffered a massive coronary. Doctors aren't sure he will make it, and if he does recover, there are no guarantees what sort of condition he will be in.

"So," she continued, "at this very difficult time for Alexei and me and the people his firm employs, I've had to jump in and take control of his affairs."

"I'm surprised you would want to get involved," Tree said.

"Why would that surprise you, Tree?"

"Given what's happened."

"Given what's happened, I feel I have no choice. Even though he was officially retired, my husband was operating various enterprises and those mustn't be neglected. I'm proceeding to do what is necessary to keep things going."

"You know he's being investigated by the FBI."

"Yes, I am aware of the challenges I'm facing. But I should point out that where the FBI is concerned, that investigation and others pertain to Alexei and have nothing to do with me, or, it should be said, with most of the businesses he controls. Earlier, I was in touch with various federal officials and made it clear that we are willing to cooperate in every possible way. If Alexei is guilty of wrongdoing, then that will come out and we will have to deal with it."

"I'm not quite sure what to think, Judy," Tree said.

"What is the confusion on your part, Tree?" Judy was sounding the way she sounded when they were in front of a lawyer getting a divorce.

Tree said, "I'm not sure whether you're out of trouble or in more of it."

"I appreciate your concern, not to mention everything you and Freddie have done for me. But you don't have to worry. That's not why I called you here."

"Why did you call me?"

"You may remember I recently gave you an envelope?"

"It's in a safe place."

"I need to get it back from you."

When Tree didn't say anything, Judy's cheery countenance darkened somewhat. "Is there a problem?"

"I hate to ask a question so often asked of me, but are you sure you know what you're doing?"

Judy said, "When do you suppose I could get that envelope from you?"

"I'd have to pick it up," Tree said.

Judy's face darkened more. "What do you mean?'"

"I just told you, it's in a safe place. I didn't leave it lying around the house. You were worried about Alexei. So was I."

"All right, but when can I get it from you?"

"As soon as I can get to it," Tree said.

"You understand, Tree, I don't want any trouble about this."

"Did I just hear something that sounds like a threat?"

Judy mustered a smile. "Don't be ridiculous. As I said before, I have nothing but appreciation for what you and Freddie did for me. I want to reassure you that I have no bad feelings about the disdainful, insulting manner in which you treated me when we were married."

"You know Rex is still in jail," Tree said.

She frowned. "Yes, but what's that got to do with anything we're talking about here?"

"Let's suppose for a moment that it does."

"I'm not sure how that could possibly be the case," Judy said.

"It wasn't so long ago that you did. You suspected your husband might have been responsible for the deaths of Kelly Fleming and Brittany Pools."

Judy's fingers touched at the edge of her newly coiffed hair. "I was distraught at the time, feeling anything might be possible."

"And now?"

"I don't know that Alexei killed those women if that's what you're getting at."

"But you are surrounded by people who might. Now you're in a position to find out the truth. Whatever Alexei did, he didn't do it in a vacuum. Find out from them what they know."

"And if I don't do this?"

"I would look at it from a slightly different perspective. Your help in proving Rex's innocence would make it a lot easier to get that envelope back."

"This is an interesting turn of events, isn't it, Tree? Now it sounds suspiciously like you're trying to blackmail me."

"Not at all," Tree said. "You're not threatening me. I'm not blackmailing you."

"So I guess we know where we stand with each other," Judy said, rising to her feet.

"Yes, I guess we do." Tree stood to face her.

"That's better," Judy said.

"Is it?"

"All the time we were married, I never knew where I stood with you. Now, finally, I do. The lines are drawn, aren't they?"

"Yes, I suppose they are," Tree said. "It turns out, there is a lot more to you than I ever imagined."

"Not really," Judy said brightly. "Nothing's changed. I'm still just plain Judy Blair, a simple Midwestern girl from southern Illinois, who married a guy who lied to her and betrayed her and her children, and then dumped her at the curb as he left for another woman."

There wasn't a trace of acrimony in words laced with it. Tree felt his throat constrict, choking his words: "I'm so sorry, Judy. Truly I am."

"Oh, Tree," she said. "You know what? I don't think you're sorry at all."

He sensed rather than saw someone behind him. He turned and, sure enough, there was the omnipresent Valentin. This time, he wasn't smiling. Judy, by contrast, looked overjoyed. She said, "Valentin, Mr. Callister is leaving." She addressed Tree. "You will get me that envelope, Tree."

Valentin followed Tree out of the sitting room and across the foyer. When they reached the door, Valentin laid a gigantic hand on Tree's shoulder. "Do me a favor." Tree looked at him. "Do not underestimate her—or me."

"Of course, Valentin. As long as you promise not to bash my head in."

"I cannot make you that promise." Valentin's small eyes were black holes boring into Tree.

Tree crossed the drive to his car. He got in and started the motor. He looked over and saw Judy in the entranceway. An overhead light cast her in gold, a golden angel at the door. An angel holding Valentin's hand.

33

That can't be Judy," Freddie said when Tree got back to Andy Rosse Lane and told her what had happened.

"It's the Judy after her rich Russian husband has suffered a heart attack and left her unexpectedly in charge," Tree said. "The Judy who it turns out is still pretty angry with me."

"Or a more duplicitous Judy than we might have imagined," Freddie countered. "Perhaps the person who has been planning something like this for some time."

"But she couldn't have imagined Alexei would have a heart attack," Tree said.

"Couldn't she? Why not? Or maybe she was already hatching plans with her pal Valentin, and the fact that Alexei got sick just made it that much easier."

"I'm having a difficult time wrapping my head around that notion," Tree said.

"It just seems hard to imagine her relationship with Valentin, if that's what it was, started the moment Alexei went into the hospital."

"But Valentin came here to get her back," Tree said.

"Like I said, the duplicitous Judy. Valentin, too. He had no choice but to try to take her forcibly. That way she could play the scared wife running away from the vicious oligarch."

Tree's cellphone began to vibrate. He swiped it open. "What's up, Tommy?"

"Thomas, Mr. Callister," Tommy Dobbs said.

"Everyone wants to be called something different, I can't keep up," Tree said.

"Listen, I just got off the phone with my editor in Chicago," Tommy said. "Senator John Hardy has given an interview saying he doesn't believe his wife committed suicide."

"What's he say happened to her?"

"He thinks she was murdered."

"Does he say who murdered her?"

"He believes Kelly killed her."

That left Tree speechless yet again. Tommy said, "Are you still there, Mr. Callister?"

"Yeah, I'm here. What are the police saying?"

"The police are dismissing the idea, and sticking by the suicide, but no surprise, it's a big story up there."

"Yes, I guess it would be."

"So Mr. Callister, they are on me to link Senator Hardy's allegations to Kelly's murder. I'd like to get a statement from you."

"What can I say, uh, Thomas. Rex Baxter didn't kill Kelly, and the fact that Senator Hardy is making these allegations about a dead woman who can't defend herself doesn't change that fact."

"You were married to Kelly Fleming, Mr. Callister. Any thoughts on whether she was capable of murder?"

"Not the Kelly, I knew. No, of course not."

"That's great, Mr. Callister. That's all I need for now. I'll be in touch."

When Tommy hung up Tree turned to Freddie and said, "You're not going to believe this."

"At this point there is nothing I wouldn't believe," Freddie said.

"Senator John Hardy now says his wife didn't commit suicide. He claims she was murdered—by Kelly Fleming."

"You're right," Freddie said. "I don't believe it."

Before he could explain further, Tree's phone sounded again. This time it was T. Emmett Hawkins. "I think we had better get together with Rex," he said.

"What's wrong?"

"Rex says he wants to plead guilty," Hawkins said.

34

Rex sat at a table across from Tree and Hawkins in an airless, windowless conference room at the Lee County Jail. Strange to see Rex in person rather than on a video monitor, Tree thought. He looked even paler, and he had lost more weight.

"I'm tired of it," Rex said in a husky voice devoid of its usual energy. "I just want this to be over."

"I want this to be over, too," Hawkins said. "But spending the rest of your life in jail is not the way to do it."

"You know for the first time I understand how they wear people down and get them to admit to crimes they didn't commit," Rex said. "You get so fed up with the system and with yourself you start to think, to hell with it, maybe I am guilty, maybe they should lock me up."

"Is that what you're thinking?" Tree asked.

Rex didn't say anything.

"Look, for what it's worth," Tree said. "I believe I'm making progress getting to the real killer."

"Yeah? What kind of progress?" Rex's gaze met Tree's. Was Tree imagining things, or had the light gone out in his old friend's eyes?

"The young woman who was cleaning your pool, Brittany Pools."

Rex's eyes narrowed. "What about her?"

"She was Miranda Hardy's daughter. Did you know that?"

Rex blinked a couple of times. "No, I didn't know that," he said.

"She's been murdered. It turns out that she was also involved with a wealthy Russian living here, Alexei Markov."

Rex looked at him in disbelief. "The guy we met who is now married to Judy?"

"That's right. I think there could be a connection between Kelly's death and Brittany's murder."

"Come on. You somehow have arrived at the notion that this guy Markov killed Kelly?"

"And then killed Brittany to keep her quiet."

"Why the hell would he murder them?"

"That's what I'm trying to figure out," Tree said. It all sounded pretty wobbly, even to Tree. Hawkins, who might have been expected to chime in at this point with assurances that Tree was onto something, said nothing.

"I just need more time," Tree said. "Give me a few more days before you do anything, Rex. Please."

That stirred Hawkins to life. "Let's at least give Tree a chance," he said. "Another week or so, see what he comes up with. That will give me an opportunity to better ascertain what the prosecution has up its sleeve. At that point we can reassess the situation and decide on next moves."

Rex was silent for a time. Then he said in a flat voice, "Supposing I'm guilty?"

"I don't want to hear that," Hawkins snapped with uncharacteristic gusto. "Let's not even go there."

Rex studied his hands clenched together on the table, not saying anything. Tree leaned forward and said, "We're going to get you out of this, Rex. We are going to do it."

Rex said, "Are you, Tree?"

"Yes, we are," Tree replied. "I promise you, Rex. Just hang in there a while longer."

"I'm so tired of it," Rex said. "I don't sleep, I can't eat. I keep thinking about how much of my life I screwed up, and now it ends with me in jail for killing the woman I loved—who never loved me. Probably didn't give a tinker's damn about me."

"Don't be ridiculous," Tree said. "If anyone screwed up his life, it's me. Not you."

Rex smiled weakly. "I seem to be the one sitting in a jail cell."

"Another week, Rex. Give me another week, please."

Rex sat back, looking exhausted. He threw up his hands. "What the hell," he said.

It was growing dark as Tree and Hawkins reached the parking lot outside the jail. What was left of the sunlight glinted off razor wire topping the surrounding fences, making it seem as though the compound was ringed with fire. Hawkins turned unhappily to Tree.

"You failed to mention to Rex that the esteemed senator from Illinois, Mr. John Hardy, now believes his wife Miranda did not commit suicide, that she was in fact murdered by none other than Kelly Fleming."

"So you know about that," Tree said.

"Of course. It's my business to know these things," Hawkins said.

"It's an irrational allegation," Tree said.

"Is it?" Hawkins said.

"He has no evidence as far as I know and besides, it doesn't change the fact that Rex is innocent. He didn't kill Kelly."

"According to the state's case, which I have now had an opportunity to take a closer look at, Rex was in Chicago seeing Kelly at the time of Miranda Hardy's death. That does open the possibility that he was an accessory to her murder. It might also bolster the state's case."

"How does it do that?"

"The prosecution could well argue that Rex murdered Kelly in order to keep her quiet about what happened to Miranda Hardy."

"This is madness," pronounced Tree.

"Nonetheless, that possibility is being explored by ADA Bixby and his minions. I am beginning to think that where this case is concerned, anything is a possibility. The least of the possibilities, I have to say, appears to be Rex's innocence."

35

After Hawkins drove away, Tree lingered behind the wheel of the Beetle. The sun was gone and with it the fiery razor wire. The Lee County Jail had regained its grim unwelcoming façade, leaving no doubt bad people were caged here. Except Rex Baxter was not a bad person. He was Tree's oldest, kindest, most reliable friend. He was not a killer. He was not guilty.

The tragedy of all this lay not with Rex inside that steel box; it was in the parking lot, behind the wheel of the Beetle, in the person of W. Tremain Callister, failed detective and friend. He had so far let Rex down. He was no closer to the real killer than some vague notion of Alexei Markov and a hazy connection between Kelly and Brittany Pools.

And now even Tree's faintest of hopes, Markov, had taken himself out of the picture by suffering a heart attack.

Or had he?

———

They were surprisingly helpful at HealthPark Medical Center, part of the Lee Memorial Hospital complex. An attendant at Visitor Information, after consulting a computer screen, said Alexei Markov had been released from intensive care. He was in a private room on the third floor.

Alexei appeared to be doing better than anyone expected, his wife included.

Tree bought a vase of assorted cut flowers in one of the shops on the main concourse and then took the elevator to the third floor. From the elevators, it was only a few steps to Markov's room. No one saw Tree enter.

Markov lay on his back. Two small nozzles attached to a tube delivered oxygen. The flickering green lines of the heart-monitor LCD screen were constant evidence that Markov lived and therefore remained a threat.

The Russian looked groggily up as Tree approached the bed holding the vase of flowers. He resembled nothing like the rich, powerful oligarch Tree had previously encountered. His stay at HealthPark had reduced him to an old man, like any other old man, unshaven, the lines in his face cut deeper than ever, the hair even more ludicrous in its disarray, poking up every which way from his skull. He squinted at Tree, not certain what he was seeing.

"What are you doing here?" he said in a slurred voice.

"I heard you weren't well, Alexei, so I brought you flowers," Tree said.

Markov looked at him in disbelief as Tree set the vase down on the bedside table near a smartphone the size of a wallet. "How are you feeling?" Tree asked.

"I feel terrible, how do you think I feel? I suppose you have come to kill me."

"Me?" Tree said. "No, Alexei, it's actually not a bad idea, I suppose, but I don't want to kill you."

"You may be the only person in the world who does not want me dead," he said.

"Is your wife on that list?"

Markov managed a small smile. "Yes, well, that's a possibility, is it not?"

"So you know what she's doing," Tree said.

"I know what she would do, given the chance. I have now given her that chance. That does not surprise me. You being here, with flowers no less, that surprises me."

"I'm looking for information," Tree said.

"Then you have wasted your time, my friend. I have no information to give you."

"An innocent man sits in jail accused of a murder he didn't commit. I think you know this. I believe you can help me get him out."

"Can I? I could bore you with my bleak philosophy that argues there are no innocent men. Only those stupid enough to get caught."

"I don't believe that," Tree said.

"Believe what you want," Markov said. "You are wasting your time here." He tried a second weak smile. "But I do like the flowers. Now please, get out. I am tired and sick and you bother me."

"Tell me what you know."

"I know that I am going to call for a nurse if you don't leave."

"That's the worst you can do, Alexei? Threatening me with a nurse? Goes to show you how far you've fallen."

On the bedside table, Markov's smartphone began to vibrate. He turned his head expectantly. "I need to take that," Markov said.

"You want me to help you, or do you want me to leave?"

"You are a bastard," Markov said. "Hand me phone."

Tree picked up the phone, swiped it and then held it to Markov's ear as he struggled to sit up. "*Da?*"

On the other end of the line, Tree could hear someone speak quickly in Russian. Man or woman? Tree couldn't make out which. Markov said, "*Kak skopo?*" More Russian followed from the other end of the line. "*Ya ponimayu,*" Markov said. He poked a thick finger at the phone, ending the call.

"Are you finished?"

"Yes," Markov said impatiently. "I am definitely finished."

Tree replaced the phone on the bedside table. Markov struggled to sit up further in bed, yanking the oxygen tube out of his nose.

"What are you doing?" Tree asked.

"Getting out of here," Markov said. "What does it look like?"

"Why would you do that?"

"Because people come to this place to kill me," he said.

"Is that what that phone call was about?"

"About trying to reassure me," Markov said. "When that happens where I come from, they are about to kill you."

"You're in a major cardiac unit in Fort Myers. No one is going to kill you here."

"How naïve you are," Markov said. He was breathing heavily, throwing back the covers. "Are you going to help me or not?"

"How can I help you?" Tree said.

"Help me out of here," Markov said. "I must leave immediately. There is very little time."

"Why should I do that?"

Markov stared at him, making loud breathing sounds. "Because then I tell you about the famous senator, my friend Mr. John Hardy."

"What do you know about him?"

"I know what you should know."

"What do you know, Alexei?"

"First, you get me out of this place. Then we talk."

Tree looked at the Russian in his wrinkled green hospital gown, mouth open, gasping for air, trying to get himself upright. "I must be out of my mind," Tree said.

"Both of us," Markov agreed. He had already pulled off the clothespin pulse oximeter attached to his finger. He shifted the hospital gown around and began to tug at the electrodes attached to his chest with sticky pads.

"Where are your clothes?" Tree said.

"No time," Markov said. "There is a wheelchair in the corner. Use that."

Tree unfolded the wheelchair and placed it beside the bed. Then he helped Markov unsteadily to his feet. He groaned and gritted his teeth. He was very pale. "Are you going to be able to do this?"

"Yes, yes," Markov said. "There is no choice."

Tree maneuvered Markov around to get him into the wheelchair, lowered the metal stirrups, got his feet into them, and then opened the door. He peered down the deserted hallway, relieved and surprised that unhooking Markov from the heart monitors hadn't alerted the nurses. Tree wheeled the Russian out of the room and pushed him the short distance to the elevators.

"Hurry," Markov hissed. "We must hurry."

36

When they got to the elevators, Tree pressed the down button and waited anxiously. He looked at Markov slumped forward in the wheelchair, wheezing through his open mouth, looking worse than ever. The elevator doors opened and Tree pushed the wheelchair into the empty compartment. The doors closed. The sound of Markov's labored breathing filled the elevator. "Are you going to be all right?"

"Fine, fine," Markov mumbled.

The elevator reached the atrium lobby. It was busier here, even at this time of night, but no one noticed another wheelchair-bound patient being pushed along.

They went outside to the parking lot, Tree beginning to wonder what they were running away from.

"Look, are you sure people are after you?" he asked Markov as he pushed him forward.

"Are you out of your mind? Of course they are after me." Markov's voice was raspy and irritated. "For now, thanks to that phone call, we are a step ahead. But that won't last. I know about these things. That is how I survive. Do you know how embarrassing this is for me? To have to rely on a man such as yourself?"

"I can imagine," Tree said.

When they arrived at the Beetle, Tree positioned the wheelchair beside the passenger door. Then he lifted the complaining Markov to his feet, his behind hanging out, the hospital gown gathered around the Russian's thighs, maneuvering him awkwardly into the car. "You are hurting me," Markov cried.

"Just relax," Tree said. "Let me get you down on the seat."

"You are an idiot," Markov announced. "How could my wife have married such a man?"

Tree positioned Markov in the passenger seat, and reached for the seat belt. Markov raised his hand to stop him. "I don't want it, too painful."

"Suit yourself," Tree said.

He went around to the driver's side and got in. The interior of the Beetle filled with the sweet-stale smell of a sick man, barely hanging onto consciousness.

"Tree turned to his passenger. "Before we go anywhere, Markov, we need to talk."

The Russian's head was back against the seat. "I am so tired," he said. "Get me out of here. We talk later."

"Let's talk about your friend, Senator John Hardy."

"Yes, the great Senator Hardy." His voice dripped sarcasm. "My friend, the senator."

"Tell me what you know," Tree said.

"I know you are a fool," Markov said. "That's all I know."

"What else, Alexei?"

"Hardy the senator. Hardy the killer."

"Who did he kill?"

"You truly are a fool. Who do you think?"

"His wife? You're saying he killed his wife?"

"I am not saying anything until you get me out of here."

"What about Kelly?"

"Drive!"

"First you talk to me," Tree said.

Markov didn't say anything. His head rolled against the seat. He looked worse than ever, Tree thought. It occurred to him he was sitting in a hospital parking lot with a dying man, and moving him like this was only hastening his demise.

Markov pointed a shaky finger at the windshield. "There..." he said. "Someone coming..."

Tree saw shadowy figures moving toward them. He started the Beetle, threw it into reverse and hit the gas pedal, sending the little car spinning backwards.

The gearshift made a terrible grinding sound as Tree shifted into first, the car lurching forward, engine protesting. Tree reached the street, glancing over at Markov. He was slumped against the passenger door, head down. "Markov, are you with me?" Tree called. No response.

Tree drove south on Tamiami Trail, picking up speed. "Markov," he called to his passenger. "I need to know where you want to go. Can you hear me?"

The Russian did not answer.

A red light at the next intersection forced him to a stop. He glanced into the rearview mirror an instant before an oncoming vehicle smashed into the Beetle.

The force of the collision slammed Tree against the steering wheel and threw Markov into the windshield. Tree had a sense of the car spinning in slow motion into the intersection. He caught a glimpse of the pickup truck an instant before it struck the Beetle, sending it spiraling off in another direction, Tree gripping the steering wheel trying to control the car, his foot jammed on the brake. Not that it did any good. The Beetle gyrated hard into a streetlight, twisting around the post, the windshield buckling, the passenger door caving in on Markov.

The ticking sound of metal settling broke the silence surrounding Tree. He managed to get his seatbelt off and then struggled to get the driver's-side door open. He managed to pry it loose enough so that he could squeeze out. A young man, owlish behind horn-rimmed glasses, helped him straighten up, wanting to know if he was all right. Tree wasn't sure about that. Not sure at all.

He made his way around to the passenger side wrapped against the light post. Jagged pieces of the car door had sliced through Markov's body. His head was thrown forward against the dashboard. Tree called to him. To his amazement, the Russian's eyes flickered and he managed to say, "The..."

In the distance, the wail of a siren. Tree said, "Alexei, it's all right. Help is coming."

"Envelope," Markov struggled with the word.

"What about the envelope, Alexei?"

"Useless."

His mouth twisted into something approximating a smile. "Don't tell Judy…"

The whine of the siren grew louder.

37

"Whiplash," pronounced young Dr. Noori.

Tree, seated on the edge of a gurney, would have nodded, except he was having trouble moving his head.

"Not to mention the cuts and bruises," Dr. Noori added.

"Yes," Tree said.

"Otherwise, it looks as if you'll survive."

"Glad to hear it," Tree said.

"You are in here a lot," Dr. Noori said.

"You've mentioned this before," Tree said. "I'm trying to do better, I really am."

"You are not succeeding very well," the doctor said.

"I'm beginning to think of you as a friend," Tree said hopefully.

"An older gentleman like yourself, you must be more careful. Or have I said that already?"

"Previously, you didn't use the term 'older gentleman'," Tree said.

"There's something else."

"Yes?"

"You know the police are outside waiting for you."

"Lately, I'm afraid I see the police almost as often as I see you."

"You don't look like a menace to society," the doctor said.

"The police might disagree with you," Tree said.

"Where do you think you went wrong?"

"I think it started when I married four times."

At that, Dr. Noori stepped back a couple of paces as if now convinced the police might be right in their assessment. He peered at Tree. "I don't think we will give you a brace," he said. "Better if we keep your neck mobile. It's painful, but the more you move your neck around, the sooner it will heal. I'd try over-the-counter painkillers first, but if they don't work I can prescribe something a little stronger."

"Thanks, doctor," Tree said.

"Are you planning any future marriages?" Dr. Noori asked.

"I don't think so," Tree said.

"Good," the doctor said. "Hopefully you can start to pull your life together, get back on the straight and narrow."

"Yes, the straight and the narrow, I'd like that," Tree said.

"I'll see you soon." Tree couldn't tell whether Dr. Noori was kidding or not.

A crowd had gathered in the waiting room outside emergency. Freddie, Tree was relieved to see, was present, accompanied by T. Emmett Hawkins. Neither of them looked happy to see him, although Freddie did come over and put her hand on his arm and ask if he was all right.

"A couple of cuts and bruises," he said in a reassuring voice.

She looked at him skeptically, as she usually did in these instances.

Also present were detectives Cee Jay Boone and Owen Markfield. They looked even less happy than Freddie and Hawkins. In addition, an assortment of uniformed officers were stationed around the room, eyes riveted to him, just in case he really was a menace to society and made a break for it.

However, given the way he was feeling, and the lateness of the hour, Tree didn't think he would be running anywhere. The few patients present at this time of night looked on, bug-eyed at the unfolding drama. Passing nurses and orderlies looked as though they could care less.

Cee Jay and Markfield closed in. Hawkins quickly placed himself between Tree and the detectives. "What are we doing here?" he demanded. Markfield scowled.

"We'd like to talk to Mr. Callister," Cee Jay said patiently.

"What do you wish to speak to my client about?" Hawkins, all innocence.

Markfield pushed in. "We're interested in knowing how he came to remove a patient from this hospital, put him in his car, and then got into an accident, resulting in the patient's death."

Hawkins turned to Tree. "I'm sure Mr. Callister would like to cooperate in any way he can. As long his attorney is present."

Cee Jay looked at Tree. "What about it, Tree?"

"I'd be glad to tell you what happened," Tree said.

Organized by the vigilant Hawkins, the pertinent parties seated themselves on the hospital's Naugahyde couches facing one another. Hawkins sat beside Tree. Cee Jay and Markfield sat on the other side of a low table filled with old copies of *Time* magazine and *Reader's Digest*. Markfield busied himself finding an empty page in his ever-present notebook. Freddie leaned against the wall, not far from Tree.

Cee Jay retained her air of quiet patience when she said to Tree, "So why don't you fill us in on what happened tonight."

Tree explained that he had gone to Alexei Markov's hospital room as part of an ongoing investigation he was conducting.

"What kind of investigation is that?" Markfield could not keep the sneer out of his voice.

"You know that I'm looking into the death of Kelly Fleming for Mr. Hawkins."

"How would Markov have anything to do with Kelly Fleming's murder?" Cee Jay asked.

"That's what I was trying to ascertain," Tree said.

"And did you?" Markfield looked up from his notebook.

"That's not pertinent, I don't think, to what we are discussing here," Hawkins interjected.

"Tell us what happened after you arrived at Mr. Markov's room." Cee Jay getting things back on track.

"Mr. Markov received a phone call. The caller spoke to him in Russian. After he hung up, Mr. Markov tried to get out of bed. He said people were coming to get him and he had to leave. He wanted me to help him. He was obviously scared, so I did as he requested, I helped him leave the hospital."

"Did you see any of these 'people' who were supposedly after him?" Markfield, again unable to disguise his disdain.

"In the parking lot, we spotted figures coming toward us," Tree said. "I got out of there, onto Tamiami Trail. That's when we were hit from behind."

"You were hit from behind?" This from Cee Jay.

"That's what caused the Beetle to go spinning into the intersection where it was hit by the second vehicle."

Cee Jay continued the questioning: "The vehicle that struck you from behind, was it driven by the people who Mr. Markov said were after him?"

"I don't think there can be any other explanation," Tree said.

"Are you sure about that?" Markfield interjected.

"How do you mean?"

"Could you have kidnapped Markov and in your haste to get away, got yourself involved in a car accident?"

"Why would I kidnap him?"

"I don't know," Markfield said. "Why would you?"

"That's enough for one night," Hawkins said. "I think it's clear that Mr. Callister was acting on behalf of my client and me. The question isn't so much *why* Mr. Callister helped a man in fear of his life—an act for which he should be applauded, I might add—but *who* was trying to kill an international figure of great controversy, the subject of an ongoing investigation by several federal agencies. I think you should be focusing your energies in that area, don't you?"

Neither Cee Jay nor Markfield said anything. Hawkins rose to his feet. "I'm very tired, and I suspect Mr. Callister is as well, given the events of the night. If there is nothing else, I'd like to get him out of here and into a bed."

"We are not finished with this," Markfield said in a menacing voice.

"Honestly, Detective Markfield, I do get tired of your constant threats," Hawkins said.

"I'm not threatening," said Markfield, threatening.

The act of standing wrenched at Tree's neck, causing him to wince. Freddie came over and placed a gentle arm around his waist. "Let's go home," she said.

"Yes," Tree said. "That's a very good idea."

38

"My neck is killing me, my ribcage hurts, my head is throbbing," Tree complained as Freddie crossed the causeway onto Sanibel Island. "I am feeling very old tonight."

"You are old," Freddie said.

"What's more, my beloved Beetle is a write-off."

"And I am trying my best not to be furious with you," Freddie said.

"Given the sorry state I'm in, your effort is appreciated," Tree said.

"However, I should add that I am having a great deal of difficulty not being furious with you."

"I understand."

"Whatever possessed you to go to the hospital in the first place?"

"Desperation," Tree admitted. "Rex wants to take the deal the prosecution is offering. We've been spinning our wheels with this whole thing. I felt I had to do something. My gut tells me Markov is involved in Kelly's death. I'm not sure how, but he's involved. I figured if I confronted him at the hospital I might get something out of him."

"But you got nothing."

"Something," Tree said.

"What?"

"He talked about his friend, Senator John Hardy. He suggested Hardy killed his wife."

"And you think what? That somehow Senator Hardy is behind all this?"

"Someone wanted him dead. It could have been Hardy. The phone call Markov received certainly spooked him. He badly wanted out of the hospital. And then someone rammed us from behind on Tamiami Trail."

"That wasn't an accident?"

"If it was, why didn't whoever hit me stick around?"

"Because it's South Florida," Freddie said. "People leave accident scenes all the time."

It had begun to rain by the time they reached home. Freddie came around the car and insisted on helping Tree out. He insisted he was all right as he clenched his teeth, wondering if he would ever again know a time when his body was not racked with pain.

Not if he kept on like this, he concluded.

Inside, Freddie lowered Tree to a sofa and then went around turning on lights, illuminating Judy seated on the easy chair in the corner. Tree jumped when he saw her, causing knifepoints of pain to jab into his neck. It took him a moment to realize she was holding a gun. In fairness, it was a tiny gun, easily missed.

Freddie didn't miss it, though. She addressed Judy in a calm voice: "You shouldn't come in here with a gun, Judy. That's not necessary."

"I want that envelope," Judy said.

39

What envelope is that?" Freddie said.

"The envelope Tree has been holding for me," Judy said.

"And you had to break in here to get it?"

"I didn't break in, Freddie," Judy said.

"Yes, I guess it's my bad. I was silly enough to give you a key."

"I don't want trouble, I really don't," Judy said. "But I need that envelope."

"You know what's happened to Alexei," Tree said, trying to match Freddie's calmness.

"I know he's dead," Judy said. "The police called me earlier."

"And you're pretty broken up about it," Tree said.

"Hardly," Judy replied. "That envelope, Tree."

"Like I told you before, I don't have it. It's not here."

"I have information you will find helpful," Judy said.

Freddie sat beside Tree, leaning forward, her body tense. "All the more reason to put that gun away. We can discuss this like adults. You want something from Tree. He wants something from you. Lots of room for negotiation."

"Bringing some of your management skills into play, are we Freddie?" Judy's tone was slightly sarcastic—more of the new, less-improved Judy.

"Just a reminder that you don't need the gun," Freddie said.

"Funny thing, I spent a lifetime never holding a gun, but lately I find it necessary, and quite comforting."

The gun remained pointed in their direction. Steadily held, Tree noted. He said, "I can get you the envelope, Judy. No problem. But first of all, tell me about John Hardy."

Judy looked surprised. "How do you know about him?"

"Alexei. Before he died."

Judy pondered this news before deciding to say, "I can tell you *something* of what I know."

"Fair enough," Tree said.

Judy took her time gathering her thoughts. Eventually she said, "Let's say that Alexei needed help in order to do business in America, the kind of help that comes from people like Hardy. Not a lot of those people wanted anything to do with him, and he was becoming pretty frustrated until he met John Hardy. The senator was willing to help, but in return he wanted the impossible. But when you know a man like Alexei, certain things you might have thought impossible become possible."

"Such as getting rid of unfaithful wives?" Freddie said.

"Yes, that would certainly be one of those things," Judy said. "It also becomes a lot easier to get rid of the woman with whom your wife is having an affair."

"That could explain how Miranda and Kelly died," Tree said. "But what about Brittany Pools?"

"Women who know too much can also be easily disposed of," Judy said.

"So Rex had nothing to do with Kelly's death," Tree said.

"Not if you believe the story I'm telling you."

"But why didn't you say something?" Freddie said.

"Because I didn't know anything—until now. These are not the kind of things Alexei discussed with me."

"How do we prove any of this?" Tree asked.

"There's a path you can pursue that takes you away from Rex, but it's up to you to pursue it." Judy rose to her feet. The gun was still in her hand. "I've already told you more than I should have. Now, I need that envelope."

"I'll get it for you tomorrow."

Judy frowned. "Is that the best you can do?"

"I'll bring it to your house first thing in the morning. That's a promise."

Judy issued a tiny laugh. "Oh, Tree. You and your promises. If I had a dollar for every one of those Tree Callister promises, I would be a rich woman." She lowered the gun she was holding. "Come to think of it, I am a rich woman." She paused for effect and then said, "I haven't told you everything, incidentally."

"No?"

"I was very foolish with you when we were married, Tree, no doubt about that. But I'm not stupid. Not where you're concerned."

"I never thought you were, Judy."

"Make sure you bring the envelope tomorrow," she said. "Then I might just tell you more."

40

A five-star hotel suite cast in shadow, French doors opening to a balcony and a view of the Riviera one pays massive sums to enjoy. An elegant blonde in a white evening dress set off by a glittering necklace, a swanlike neck and faultless jawline, glittering blue eyes trained on Tree Callister.

"I have a feeling that tonight you're going to see one of the Riviera's most dazzling sights," the elegant blonde said.

Tree looked at her. She smiled back and raised a slim hand holding an envelope. "I was referring to the envelope," she said.

"In the movie, it's the necklace you're wearing."

"But this isn't the movie, is it, Tree?"

"Then what is it?"

"Another of your long-held fantasies," she said. "You are awed by my icy beauty."

"I am?"

"But even I can't stop you obsessing over this envelope and what's in it. We both want to catch our thieves, don't we, Tree? What's inside may help you to catch yours."

They were interrupted by fireworks shooting into the sky outside. He sat beside her on the sofa.

She said, "Hold the envelope in your hand and tell me you don't want to look inside and see what's in it."

"I have the same interest in what's in that envelope as I have in horse racing, politics, modern poetry, or women who need weird excitement. None."

"Now you're quoting from the movie," she said. "That's not really what you're thinking."

"Isn't it?"

"Your former wife has provided a solution of sorts to the mystery. All she wants in return is this envelope. Strange, isn't it? If her late husband orchestrated the murders of Kelly Fleming and Brittany Pools, not to mention Miranda Hardy in Chicago, then what's she want the envelope for? What's in there?"

The exploding fireworks lit the darkened room in a rainbow of colors.

The elegant blonde said, "Convenient, don't you think? A dead Russian killed everyone. It all fits nicely together, doesn't it?"

"Or maybe it doesn't," Tree said.

"Of course it doesn't," said Frances. "None of it is real. Not me, not the fireworks, and not what you're being told."

The envelope in her hand burst into flame. More fireworks exploded outside, framing the elegant blonde in white light as she held the burning envelope, distracted by a tapping sound.

"What's that?" She looked perplexed.

"I don't know," Tree said, equally confused.

Tree jerked awake. Todd Jackson's face loomed in the driver's side window. He tapped the glass again. Tree sat up and rolled down the window of the Mercedes.

"Sorry, I'm late," Todd said.

"I must have dozed off," Tree said.

He got out, squinting into the morning sun shining on the Tahitian Mall. Todd's truck was nearby with its distinctive chalk body outline and big printed letters that said SANIBEL BIOHAZARD.

The two men embraced before Todd handed him the envelope.

"Thanks for hanging onto this," Tree said.

"No problem, particularly if it helps Rex. I was around to see him yesterday."

"How's he doing?"

"Not great, but that's hardly a surprise. A man his age shouldn't be sitting in a jail cell. He's pretty broken up, talking about giving up on the whole thing. I told him not to say too much because they're probably recording all inmate conversations. But it's hard to keep him quiet."

"We're going to get him out of there," Tree said.

"That's what I told him," Todd said. He pointed to the envelope Tree was holding. "Is that going to help?"

"Let's see," Tree said.

He tore open the envelope. Inside were ten sheets of paper written in what appeared to be Russian. "Well, that's not a lot of help," Tree said after leafing through the pages.

"What is that? Russian?"

"Looks like it," Tree said.

Todd grinned. "I've got a guy on my team. Serge. He's from the Ukraine, but he speaks Russian."

———

Todd's Biohazard team was working in a rundown house on Hanson Avenue where a forty-year-old man had shot himself in the head a couple of days before.

Serge was all but lost in his white hazmat suit. He came out of the house into the backyard, removed his breathing apparatus to reveal a round, flushed face dotted with perspiration. "Is hot work," Serge commented. Todd handed him a bottle of water. Serge took a long swig as Todd explained what he would like Serge to do.

"Sure, I look, no problem," he said.

Tree took out the sheaf of papers from the envelope. Serge removed the blue gauntlet-type gloves he wore while working and then took the papers. Serge's brow curled as he read through them, handing each page back to Tree as he finished it.

Finally, he shrugged and looked up at Tree and Todd. "Not sure," he said.

"Not sure of what?" Todd demanded. "You're not sure what's in them or you're not sure what they mean?"

"Maybe both," stated Serge. "It's official document. Like agreement or something."

"For what?" Tree asked.

"Looks like for house. On Sanibel."

41

Sanibel, ah my Sanibel, Tree thought as he drove along Periwinkle Way, moonlit nights in paradise, an endless sun, everything out in the open.

Well, maybe not quite.

So much could be hidden under the moon or in the sunshine, down little-known roads twisting through mangroves into secret places. Sanibel allowed you to present yourself as one thing and at the same time hide something else entirely in plain, sunny view.

In a house, for example. Not too far away. With easy access. So that there was no inconvenience. A house smaller than expected, hidden in the shadows of the surrounding trees, worn awnings over the front windows, in need of a coat of paint. Tree parked his car at the edge of the gravel roadway a couple of hundred yards past the house.

He walked back to where a black Toyota SUV was parked. Its front was smashed in, a headlight broken. He went past it to the faded blue front door, considered knocking, rejected the idea, and pressed the latch. The front door opened smoothly. Tree stepped into a cool interior, sunlight from the floor-to-ceiling windows, the soft hush of an air conditioner, a voice from a radio in the other room, NPR's *Fresh Air* concerned with the worsening crisis in…where? The source of the crisis would not be known, the voice with that information abruptly cut off.

A tall woman holding a cup of coffee wearing a thin white robe falling just past her thighs stepped into view. She looked vaguely surprised when she saw Tree. She recovered quickly and said in accented English, "It's early in the morning for visitors. I'm just getting out of bed."

"It's not that early," Tree said.

"Well, early for me. And you have me at a disadvantage. I wasn't expecting company. I hardly have anything on."

Which did not seem to upset her in the least.

"Yes, I can see that," Tree said.

"You look quite familiar. Do I know you?"

"The last time I saw you, you were trying to get a Porsche through a pair of closed gates."

She smiled knowingly. "Yes, I remember now. My knight in shining armor, trying to save me from terrible Valentin."

"That's me," Tree said.

"Have you come to save me again?"

"Or maybe this time you can save me," Tree said.

"I was so angry that day," she said.

"How are you this morning?"

"Not nearly so angry now that my knight has arrived, but wondering why you have come."

"Looking for you," Tree said.

She issued a half smile. "Well, it depends on who you are looking for, doesn't it?"

"Elin Danielsen," Tree said.

"Then you have found me," she said.

She was much as she was the first time Tree saw her, those high cheekbones and prominent breasts. This morning the light was more revealing, accenting the fine web of lines around her eyes and mouth, hints her beauty was not quite ageless.

"Although," she continued, "you have me at a disadvantage, I'm afraid. You know who I am, but I have no idea who my knight is."

"I don't think that's true," Tree said. "I think you know who I am."

She considered this and then smiled again. You couldn't help but like that smile, Tree thought. Dangerous business liking that smile. "Humor me," she said.

"I'm Tree Callister."

Her green eyes lit with understanding. "The ex-husband of that woman."

"Better known as Alexei's wife," Tree said.

"She was never really his wife. That was a joke."

"A joke you tolerated," Tree said.

"Some things must be accommodated. Realities faced. Judy was one of those realities. I never understood Alexei, why he married her." She made a face. "He thought it was necessary. What can you do? Alexei said you were some sort of detective. An amateur. Not very good, he said."

"You're probably right," Tree said. "For instance, I thought I'd found the clue to the mystery I've been trying to get to the bottom of."

"A mystery? How fascinating."

"It just goes to show you what kind of detective I am," Tree said. "You see, it turned out not to be a clue at all. Actually, Markov told me it was worthless. I suppose I should have listened to him."

"What was this clue you talk about?"

"Just a document written in Russian, official papers, specifying that you own this house."

"You are right. That doesn't seem like much of a clue."

"It meant something to Judy. She thought she needed it. Maybe she was just trying to tie up all the loose ends."

"It is good to see you again, Tree Callister, but really, I don't understand why you would be looking for me."

"My best friend in the world is in jail for something he didn't do, and I've been trying to prove him innocent."

"And have you had any success?"

"Yes, as a matter of fact I have."

"Good for you," Elin said.

"I know that Alexei had Miranda Hardy murdered and Kelly Fleming, too. He probably got his man Valentin to do the actual dirty work—make it look like suicide in the one case. He might have wanted to do the same thing with Kelly, too, but it got botched, and my friend Rex ended up being arrested."

Elin didn't seem at all surprised. "What has any of this got to do with me?"

"I'm pretty sure Alexei was responsible for the murders, but now that he's dead, there's no proof. I think you can provide me with the proof I need."

"How am I supposed to do that?"

"I'm guessing you knew what Alexei was doing. Your testimony could convince the police that Rex is innocent."

Elin put her coffee cup on the counter, keeping her eyes fixed on Tree, a smile playing at the corners of her mouth. "It is far too early in the morning for all this wonderful fiction that you are weaving. You must give me a chance to wake up more so that I can enjoy it."

"Try this on for size," Tree said. "You knew about the murders and so if you didn't know before, you came to know what Alexei was capable of, and you began to worry, particularly since you also knew about his money-laundering activities, his association with Tal Fiala. The FBI was on to Tal and coming after Alexei and that was of great concern to him, so much so that he even had Brittany Pools killed because he probably thought she knew too much. All this made you think that you might be next on Alexei's hit list."

"Yes, of course, how could these things not cross a person's mind?" Elin said.

"Then, out of the blue, salvation of sorts. Alexei had a heart attack and it looked as though he was finished. You were safe. His wife might be a problem, but then maybe not. Valentin was in her bed, but what was that, convenience? At least on his part? You thought you could lure him away, and that probably turned out not to be hard at all."

"I am enjoying this," Elin said. "You are making me sound so delightfully manipulative."

"But even with Valentin on your side, there were still doubts. After all, with Alexei, you could never be certain. The monster was weakened, but he might rise again. For the moment, however, there was opportunity. The question was, could you take advantage of that opportunity?"

"This is fascinating," she said. "Please go on." Her startlingly opaque green eyes watched him carefully, revealing nothing.

"You and Valentin decided to finish him at the hospital. Otherwise, he might actually recover and then where would you be? But a couple of things went wrong. I showed up unexpectedly, and then somebody phoned to warn him, maybe Judy. Alexei further surprised you when he used me to try to escape. Thanks to that SUV in the drive, he didn't get away."

"You may not be much of a detective," Elin said. "But you tell marvelously inventive stories."

"Here is the best part, Elin. I don't have to tell the cops any of it. For all they know, I'm the stupid detective who kidnapped Alexei from his hospital bed and got him killed in a hit-and-run accident."

"And what must I provide in return for this generous silence on your part?"

"All you have to do is tell the police what you know about Alexei."

"That's it?"

"That's more than enough to get Rex out of jail."

She straightened up from the counter. "There is no rush," she said.

"Actually, there is. Do we have a deal or not?"

"Yes, Alexei is all the things you say he is, and I could be persuaded to talk to the police."

Sunlight flooded the kitchen and burst through the thin robe, illuminating Elin's superb figure. Fantasy becoming reality, the lines blurring as Elin moved toward him, saying something. What was she saying?

"There's no reason why we cannot reach, how do you call it here? An accommodation?"

"Like you said, some things must be accommodated, Elin."

"Of course, that is the way of the world, is it not?" She reached out to him, slim fingers touched at his face. "Would you like something to drink? It's not too early, is it? We can have a drink together, relax, and discover that accommodation and afterward I could talk to the police about Alexei."

Tree smiled. "Funny, I used to have dreams like this when I was a kid. Inspired, I suppose, by all those pulp-fiction detective novels I read back then."

"Sometimes, dreams can become pleasant reality," she said in a husky voice.

"Like right now, I suppose."

"Why not?" Elin said.

"You know what? I'm all grown up, and all too aware dreams seldom have anything to do with reality."

"A shame," Elin said. "It might have been fun." She smiled and took her hand away.

He caught a glimpse of someone behind him. Valentin, naked, coming from the bed he must have been sharing with Elin when Tree arrived. A thin wire stretched between balled fists. Tree got his hand up an instant before Valentin could wind the garrote around his neck.

The wire cut into the soft muscles in the edge of his hand. Blood spurted out in a long stream, splashing the front of Elin's robe. She gasped.

Valentin whipped him around, Elin crying out something in—what?—Swedish? Russian? Tree flailed against Valentin, a block of marble and as hard to move. The pain in his hand was excruciating. Valentin made grunting sounds as he tried to get the wire off Tree's hand, all that was blocking access to Tree's windpipe.

The gunshot sounded like a cannon going off. Valentin loosened his grip on the garrote. A second shot and the wire became loose, hanging from the deep bloody gash in Tree's hand. He collapsed to the floor as Valentin lurched forward, Judy following behind him, face set, her pocket pistol in her outstretched hand.

The wounded block of marble that was Valentin crashed through the window. The streaming sunlight framed Elin in shock turning to Judy now pointing the gun at her.

Tree had just enough wherewithal to call out, "Judy, don't." Not very effective, he dimly surmised, but it caused Judy to pause.

"I followed him here," Judy said to no one in particular. "I suspected he was seeing her, and sure enough." Her eyes locked on Elin. "You betrayed everything, took Valentin away,"

"Better do something, Callister," Elin said in a preternaturally calm voice. "If she shoots me, your friend is liable to spend the rest of his life in jail."

Tree said to Judy, "Listen to me, please. I need Elin alive. Right now, you've saved my life—self-defense. If you shoot her, it's murder. It's not worth it, Judy."

"Maybe it is," Judy said.

"You are fat and old," Elin sneered. "What do you expect? Valentin used you. He loved me. Just like Alexei."

"Judy, don't listen to her, put the gun down, help me free Rex."

I don't know if I want to do that," Judy said in a trembling voice.

"Look at me," Tree said. "I'm bleeding all over the place. If you don't call an ambulance pretty soon, I'm going to bleed to death."

Judy hesitated a moment longer, and then she began to scream, a sound coming from deep in her throat, an animal cry, equal parts frustration and anger. As she screamed out, she threw the gun at Elin who ducked and started yelling back.

A cacophony of noise as he faded: two women in simultaneous fury, shards of glass dropping around the unmoving Valentin, police sirens overwhelming everything.

And then he was gone.

42

"I really don't know what to say to you," Dr. Noori said when he finally finished stitching and bandaging Tree's wounded hand.

"There's probably nothing more to say at this point," Tree said. "It's all been said."

"I understand that, certainly. Still, I feel like I should be doing something, saying something that inspires you to rethink your life so that you're not coming in here all the time."

"I would say recent events have inspired me to want to change," Tree said. "I'm considering taking up smoking. It's probably a lot safer."

Dr. Noori didn't appear to think that was very funny. He helped Tree sit up on the gurney. The painkillers had numbed the hurt in his hand to the point where it was just about manageable.

"Once again there are a lot of police waiting for you outside."

"I'm afraid that's right."

"You really are a dangerous fellow, I've concluded."

"I'm trouble," Tree said, "looking for a place to happen."

Tree slid off the gurney. The room swirled and tilted around him. Dr. Noori held him. "Are you going to be all right?"

"You tell me," Tree said.

"You should take it easy for a while—a long while."

"First I have to face the music out there," Tree said.

"What are you going to say to them?"

"I'm going to tell them that, as unlikely as it seems, my first wife saved my life."

"Your first wife? That's right. I remember. You have been married many times."

"Four," Tree said. "Four times."

"I've been thinking about you a lot," Dr. Noori said.

"Wondering how I can get myself so banged up so often?"

"No. Wondering how it is possible for a man to be married four times."

"I have no idea," Tree said.

"It is a life of failure, I imagine," said Dr. Noori.

"It is indeed," Tree said. "It is indeed."

———

It was late. He held a glass of milk in his hand. How was that? What was he doing with a glass of milk? He never drank milk, not anymore. He came down steps into the piazza, the Trevi Fountain aglow in the night. Wait a minute. The Trevi Fountain? In Rome? How did he end up at the Trevi Fountain holding a glass of milk?

Neptune in marbled omnipotence stared down at him, flanked by a pair of Tritons managing unruly winged horses. The cascading water representing the aqueduct, the original inspiration for the fountain, poured down upon a woman with long blond hair, voluptuous breasts barely restrained in black.

She lifted her head, a sculpted rival for the marble figures above, her eyes closed as if lost in a dream. He stopped at the edge of the fountain, watching in wonder. The woman opened her eyes, saw him and smiled eagerly. "Marcello, it's me, Sylvia," she called. "Come and join me."

Yes, of course. Sylvia. So here it was, he thought, finally confronting his ultimate adolescent fantasy. A man with a glass of milk wading into the Trevi Fountain toward the Sylvia of his youthful erotic dreams. He reached her and the water poured down on them as his fingers lingered on the softness of her face. Was it ever possible she could be real? Was anything real?

The water abruptly cut off. A gray dawn light lit the piazza. The woman in black looked sad, taking his hand and leading him slowly out of the fountain.

"Where are we going?" he said to her.

"I'm letting you go," she said. "It's the end of dreams."

"The milk?" a voice said.

"The milk?" Tree, stopped, confused. He let go of the woman's hand. Her fingers touched pillowy lips, throwing him a final kiss.

The voice said, "What are you doing with a glass of milk?"

Tree looked down at his hand. Sure enough, he was holding the glass in an apartment looking out on a panoramic view of...where? Chicago? Yes, it had to be Chicago.

"I thought you were a hard-drinking newspaperman," the voice said.

"That's me," Tree agreed, looking at the glass, wondering what this was all about.

"Trust you to come to a dinner party with a glass of milk." The voice now belonged to a matronly woman swathed in wintery brown. She turned to someone behind her and said, "Fredryka, this is the guy I warned you about meeting tonight."

And this dazzling woman stood in front of him. She wore a gray mini-dress that showed off long legs in black stockings. She had the loveliest green eyes he had ever seen.

"I suppose," he said, "you're wondering what I'm doing with a glass of milk."

"What milk?"

And sure enough, he no longer held the milk. He said, "I had a glass of milk in my hand."

"Well, you don't."

"You're like a dream," he said.

"That's where you're wrong," she responded.

"I am?"

"Yes, you are, Tree. I'm not a dream. I'm the real deal. I'm not lounging on a brass bed or enticing you into the Trevi

Fountain or any of your other adolescent fantasies. You're an adult now, and I'm what you get when you start acting like an adult and give up fantasy, not to mention the failed marriages."

She was very close to him, green eyes sparkling. "I'm better than any fantasy."

"Yes," he said.

He put his arms around her. Her lips touched his, and she said, "Tree, Tree, wake up."

He opened his eyes and he was in his own bed, entwined with Freddie. "You were dreaming again," she said.

"Crazy dreams," he said.

"It's probably the painkillers they gave you. How are you feeling?"

"Sleepy, dopey. You were in the dream, incidentally."

"What was I doing?"

"Making sure I knew you are real."

"That's true," Freddie said. "But you already know that."

"Yes, I do," he said. "You've put up with a lot lately."

"I certainly have," Freddie said.

"Not everyone would put up with one ex-wife, let alone three."

"More importantly, I've also had to deal with a husband who keeps trying to get himself killed."

"It's not me," Tree said. "It's other people. They're the ones who keep trying."

"I suppose I can't get too angry with you," Freddie said. "After all, it was for a good cause."

"Yes," Tree said, fighting to keep his eyes open. "A very good cause."

He nestled closer, enfolding her, drawing her to him, the real deal, he thought as he drifted off, loving and feeling loved.

Safe home.

43

Dust covered Tree's desk in what used to be his office at the Chamber of Commerce Visitors Center. The photograph of a bikini-clad beauty catching a marlin from the days when bikini-clad beauties were thought to catch marlins and lure visitors to island paradises like Sanibel still hung on the wall.

Why had he never removed that picture? Tree wondered, seated at his desk. Lazy, he supposed. Or too busy? Hardly. Most of the time the Sanibel Sunset Detective Agency was a study in lethargy. It was those moments when it was no longer a study that got him maimed and nearly killed.

Rex appeared in the doorway with two lattes. "When did you get back?"

"Last night," Tree said.

"I hope there was a good turnout," Rex said.

"I thought there would be more people there, I guess," Tree said. "Kelly was such a fixture on the local news."

"It was another time," Rex said. "People forget."

"Nobody from the old gang showed, but then I guess there's not much of the old gang left."

"No, there isn't."

"Kelly's sister put the memorial together. She did a nice job. She asked about you."

"Probably just as well I wasn't there," Rex said.

"Sure, I understand. It was nice. I just wish more people had shown up."

"How's your hand?" Rex placed one of the lattes on the desk in front of Tree.

"This place needs a dusting," Tree said.

"It needs an occupant," Rex said, seating himself across from Tree. He had lost a lot of weight during his time in jail. But a few days on board his boat, the *Former Actor II*, had tanned his face and returned his healthy sheen.

Tree raised his bandaged left hand. "It still hurts," Tree said.

"What you did for love," Rex said.

"And I'm not going to make a big deal about my broken ribs that still hurt and my head that continues to ache. I'm not going to tell you about my uninjured body parts because I don't think there are any."

"I appreciate your stoicism," Rex said. "And it goes without saying how much I appreciate what you did for me."

"I don't know that it has to go without saying," Tree said. "You can shower me with heartfelt compliments. I can handle it."

"Instead of compliments, why don't I just let you have your office back at the same rent as you were paying before?"

"I wasn't paying any rent," Tree said.

"The return of the Sanibel Sunset Detective," Rex said. "Why not? The office is here waiting for you, and after all, even when you were supposedly retired, you still managed to get yourself into all sorts of hot water. You might as well get paid for it."

"Pay?" Tree arranged a surprised look. "Are you supposed to get paid for this?"

"It's something you might keep in mind if you decide to restart the agency. Now that Freddie is retired and everything."

"I got off the phone with T. Emmett Hawkins a few minutes ago," Tree said.

"You're changing the subject."

"You know he's representing Judy."

"That's what I heard," Rex said. "What does he think will happen to her?"

"According to Hawkins, the district attorney's office is still trying to figure that out. She and Elin are both cooperating with the FBI, so Hawkins thinks that will keep Judy out of jail, and maybe Elin, too—that and the fact that both women can afford the best legal defense available."

"I still can't come to terms with the fact that Judy, of all people, got mixed up with a Russian oligarch, and somehow managed to stickhandle herself past a couple of murders to inherit a fortune."

"Nobody is more surprised than I am," Tree said. "I can't believe we have all ended up where we ended up. Who would have thought a Chicago weatherman, a hard-drinking reporter, and a quiet housewife, who only wanted to raise kids and prepare dinner for a husband who came home on time, would end up on this island in this much trouble."

"You're forgetting Pat," Rex said.

"Skye," Tree amended. "How could I ever forget her? Ever since the Palm Beach district attorney decided not to press charges, she's been calling me."

"What does she want?"

"She's got a new lawyer. They are suing the Palm Beach Police and the district attorney's office for wrongful arrest. She says she needs a private detective to help them prove their case."

"You see? Everyone needs a private detective. Which brings me back to my original question."

"Your original question was about my hand."

"Okay, what do you think about moving back into you old office?"

"Like I said, the place needs a dusting."

"Then come back and dust it."

"Are you going to be here?"

"Why wouldn't I be?"

"After everything that's happened?"

Rex said, "I believe the best way to put all this behind me is to put all this behind me and get back to work. The board says it wants me to stay on, and when I think about it, I really don't have anything other than this island and the people on it who, more or less, stuck by me in my time of trouble."

"I don't think anyone really thought you were guilty," Tree said.

"You didn't, and that counted for more than you'll ever know," Rex said.

"Don't go all misty on me," Tree said.

"Don't worry about that," said Rex. He picked up his coffee.

"Can I be totally honest with you?"

"Go ahead." Rex sipped at his coffee.

"There were moments when it crossed my mind that you might be guilty."

"Understandable," Rex said. "After all, I was sitting in jail, charged with murder."

"But Freddie never wavered," Tree said. "Freddie always believed in you. Freddie kept me going."

"Well, you know me, Tree," Rex said, "much better than Freddie ever could. You know what I would do and what I wouldn't do."

"You certainly wouldn't kill someone you loved," Tree said.

"But you thought for a moment that I might," Rex said.

"A moment."

"But it crossed your mind," Rex said.

"Rex, I never seriously thought…"

"Just that a lot of people underestimate you, Tree," Rex said. "You've got a keen mind when all is said and done, not to mention the suspicious nature of an old-time newsman."

"I'm not sure what you're getting at."

"Who says I'm getting at anything? Maybe I'm just giving you a compliment."

Rex got to his feet, holding his coffee. "Like I said, you know me—better than anyone. The guy everyone knows but doesn't know, hail fellow well met and all that crap; the guy who goes home at night and sits alone staring out the window, watching crummy television. The guy who got something he wanted for years, finally seeing the end of the loneliness, then realizing he didn't have it and never had it to begin with, and the loneliness was a freight train coming back."

"Yes, I know you," Tree said. "I know you would never hurt someone even if they hurt you."

"Hey, you can lie to everyone else, old friend, but don't lie to me. You said it yourself; you were suspicious. You shook off those suspicions, and thank God you did. But they were there."

"Not anymore," Tree said.

"No? What did you think when you allowed your mind to drift into those dark places, Tree? Did you think, well, it could have been an accident, something Rex didn't mean to do—the last thing. But for a moment when Rex saw Kelly again he wasn't himself. You'd seen that side of him before and maybe that memory came back to you. Maybe you were thinking that in the blink of an eye Rex could be someone else, someone darker, someone who had lost something and wasn't going to get it back, and that's all it took."

"Rex," Tree said.

"But then you would think, no, that side of Rex, the side only Tree Callister ever really saw, that side was gone a long time ago. If he did something, acted in a way he shouldn't, how could he ever live with himself? How could he? Right, Tree? Am I right?"

Tree looked at him. Rex went out the door. Tree sat at his dusty desk. He stared at the bikini-clad beauty in the photograph happily catching a marlin.

He stared for a long time.

Acknowledgments

By the time I met Elizabeth Taylor she was middle-aged and, as they say, pleasantly plump, living in Washington, married to Senator John Warner, and supposedly more or less retired. Signs of the youthful beauty that had adorned dozens of movies since she was a little girl, and helped to fuel a million tabloid headlines, could be still found in the midst of that round face, and those trademark violet eyes had not lost their sparkle.

At the same time, though, it was hard to reconcile this matronly woman draped in a white caftan dress with the sensual, voluptuous object of youthful fantasy. But then reality is never going to live up to youthful fantasy. That is the whole idea behind fantasy. It is always perfect; real life never is.

Marilyn Monroe died at the age of thirty-six, but I still clearly remember the shock of her death arriving on the front page of the afternoon newspaper in 1962. Elizabeth Taylor made the mistake of getting old; Marilyn Monroe didn't and so she remains an ageless icon, her face and figure reproduced everywhere—at the Palm Beach Jewelry, Art and Antique Show featured in the novel, and even on the wall of our Fort Myers apartment where an oil portrait of an eternally lovely Marilyn occupies a place of prominence.

Although the two women were adored and desired by millions—desire being a necessary job description for actresses in those days—both were famously unsuccessful when it came to relationships. Marilyn married and divorced three times and was all alone when she died. Elizabeth was married a remarkable eight times to seven husbands (twice to Richard Burton), and although her children were with her at the end, no husband was in sight.

Even a naïve kid growing up in small town Canada lusting after both women could not help but notice the disconnect: how you could be so loved and yet be unable to find love.

Questions of love and desire haunt Tree Callister throughout *The Four Wives of the Sanibel Sunset Detective*. Tree is no stranger to failed relationships having been married four times himself. I drew inspiration from the actor Henry Fonda, who, when I talked to him, still couldn't get over the fact that he had failed at four of his five marriages. The complications of relationships remained a mystery to him, as they do to Tree, as they do to most of us, I suppose.

I married twice, but I was single for ten years between marriages and remember being in a state of perpetual confusion during much of that time. Why was I attracted to someone who wasn't attracted to me? Why was someone attracted to me and yet I wasn't interested? The mysteries of the heart, unsolvable.

Thankfully, in the writing of this novel and in attempting to come to terms with some of those mysteries, I had, as usual, a great deal of help.

First and foremost, thanks to my wife, Kathy, who makes life so endlessly wonderful and who has helped me solve many mysteries of life and love. Because of her I learned a simple truth: when two people love and respect one another, there are no mysteries. You love each other, you both care, and therefore you can work out just about anything together. It is no more complicated than that. The trouble starts when only one of you cares. It took me just forty years to figure that out.

Thanks, too, to the editors whose job it is to remind the author not of the wonders of his life, but of his many shortcomings. They are particularly adept at this and thus these novels are much better than they would be otherwise. David Kendall in Canada, Ray Bennett in London, England, and Susan Holly on Sanibel Island, Florida, all made invaluable contributions.

In Milton, the very talented Jennifer Smith orchestrated the design of the cover art while once again my indispensable brother, Ric Base of Fort Myers, patiently and with great professionalism, helped in a million different ways to bring *The Four Wives* into reality. And finally, I must acknowledge The Driver, Kim Hunter, who, recognizing my bestselling author status, once again this year drove me to Florida in his pickup truck.

Turn the page to read an excerpt from the next
Tree Callister adventure

THE SANIBEL SUNSET DETECTIVE
GOES TO LONDON

Private detective Tree Callister and his wife, Freddie,
discover that even in London, England,
they can't avoid trouble.
And murder!

1

A bicycle rider discovered the body in the bushes near a pathway winding through Meanwhile Gardens. The path led to the Grand Union Canal behind Trellick Tower where Tree Callister and his wife, Freddie Stayner, had taken an apartment.

The apartment Tree and Freddie would occupy for a month was on the twenty-seventh floor of a building that, depending on your view, was either a grim, Stalinist-era monstrosity or an art deco masterpiece imprisoned in a German expressionist nightmare by Fritz Lang.

Tree thought he and Freddie were moving into Notting Hill, but, as he usually was when it came to geography, he was wrong.

Trellick Tower was actually located in the Royal Burrough of Kensington and Chelsea. But it was just a couple of blocks away from Portobello Road, another London landmark, one, if you listened to the locals, was quickly disappearing as developers gobbled up more and more of traditional London in order to increase its appeal, not to mention expense, for the rich moving in from all over the world.

But Trellick Tower so far had survived the wealth invasion more or less intact. Like most things in London, the building came with history. Its design rose out of the imagination of the Hungarian architect Ernő Goldfinger—and yes, Tree had already learned, author Ian Fleming got into a discussion with Goldfinger's cousin on the golf course and the next thing the author titled his latest novel, *Goldfinger.*

Freddie's brother, Hale, had found the apartment for them. It featured sliding glass doors opening onto a balcony and a stunning view of London. Freddie was already in love with it, particularly since the single bedroom was dominated by a queen-size Hastens, one of the most expensive beds on the market, not to mention one of the most comfortable.

Tree and Freddie had come to London to attend the wedding of Freddie's nephew, Derek Stayner. Freddie had not seen Derek since he was a child, and Tree had never met him, but Hale, a retired American investment banker living in Golders Green, wanted the whole family together for Derek's marriage to—well, whomever Derek was marrying. Who was Derek marrying? Good question. Nobody seemed to know much about her. There was a name, Katrina Phillips, but not much more than that. Hale said she was beautiful. She worked in London, but at what precisely wasn't known. A mystery woman was the way Hale summed her up over the phone. He didn't sound very happy about it. A mystery woman loved by Derek. "Whatever love is," Hale added.

"Now Hale," Freddie said. "That's no way to talk."

"It is the talk of a man who has been through the mill three times, and is exhausted by the experience, never mind a whole lot poorer."

"Tree's been married four times, and he's not cynical," Freddie said.

"He's probably lying," replied Hale. "Besides, in the end, he got you. Goodness knows how he managed that being—well, what is he? Some sort of detective on an island off the west coast of Florida? What's that all about? Under the circumstances, I would say he may not be cynical, but he is damned lucky."

"Tree is a very good detective," Freddie said. "Too good, in fact. I'm hoping that bringing him to London means he stays out of trouble for the next month or so."

"Then hurry over, my dear sister," Hale said. "We will figure all this out when you get here."

And so they came.

"Hurry and get dressed," Freddie said. "Hale is sending a car around so that we can have lunch together at his house. You're far too engrossed in these London tabloids."

Tree sighed and put his copy of *The Sun* to one side. "There's a report today about a member of the House of Lords videotaped snorting coke and cavorting with a couple of prostitutes," Tree said. "Lord Justin Butler has resigned. The London political world is in an uproar. In the U.S. most politicians only do dull things like misuse tax payer money. They are much more interesting here."

"You're a voyeur," Freddie said.

"Politicians and hookers," Tree said. "Who can resist?"

"I'm going to leave you here if you don't hurry," Freddie said.

"I don't think Hale likes me," Tree said.

"That's not true," Freddie said. "I couldn't resist you. How could he?"

"He doesn't think I'm rich enough for you."

"You're not rich at all," Freddie said with a grin.

"You married a poor, underpaid Chicago newspaper reporter," Tree said.

"Who promptly lost his job, moved to Sanibel Island, became a detective and got himself shot—twice."

"No wonder Hale doesn't like me," Tree said.

"Get dressed," Freddie replied, "before I shoot you."

———

"What's that going on down there?" Freddie said as Tree used the two separate keys required to lock the door to their apartment. She was peering out the windows that ran the length of the passageway.

"Going on where?" Tree finished locking the door.

"Down by the canal."

Tree followed her pointed finger. Sure enough, far below, tiny figures darted around police and emergency vehicles. More tiny figures moved back and forth along the Grand Union Canal. It was a scene with which Tree was all too familiar in North

America, a scene he never imagined he would have to witness in stately, law-abiding London. Tree liked to think the citizens here behaved themselves, except in British police TV dramas. Invariably those dramas presented middle-aged police inspectors who were always polite and solved the crime by finding the flaw in the timeline that led to the clue that identified the killer. All very genteel.

Nothing at all like rough, tough, gun-crazy Florida crime.

They went through the fire doors into a blue-tiled foyer. A sign beside the elevators warned that the miscreant who had been spitting on the floor had now been identified via recently-installed CCTV security cameras. Thus if he knew what was good for him, he had better stop spitting on the floor.

"You have been warned," Freddie said.

"I will try to do better," Tree said.

The elevator doors opened and a politely disembodied English voice announced, "The doors are opening."

"In case you didn't know," Freddie said.

Tree said, "These are my kind of people. I need all the help I can get."

"Doors are closing," the voice said.

And, sure enough, they were.

"What time are we supposed to meet Hale?" Tree asked when they reached the ground floor lobby.

"Any moment now," Freddie said. "He's sending a car for us."

"I'm impressed," Tree said, "although where your brother is concerned, I'm not surprised. It's sort of his style, isn't it?"

"Hale has too much money," Freddie said.

"In London, I don't think it's possible to have too much money," Tree said.

When they came out onto Golborne Road there was no car waiting, but there were two female London police officers in yellow vests.

The older of the two women stepped forward and said, "Excuse me, do you have a moment?"

Tree and Freddie came to a stop.

"We're making inquiries in the neighborhood," the older police officer continued. "I wonder if we might ask you a couple of questions."

"Yes, of course," Freddie said. "What's happened?"

"A body has been found in the area," the officer said.

"In the park," Freddie said.

Both police officers stiffened. "Yes, how did you know that?"

"We saw the police and emergency vehicles from our apartment," Freddie said.

"Did you see anything else, anything at all out of the ordinary?"

"I'm afraid not. We've only just arrived from America."

"Then we won't keep you. Thanks for your time."

"The body you found," Freddie said. "Is it a man or a woman?"

The older police officer hesitated before she said, "I'm afraid it's a man."

"I'm so sorry," Freddie said.

The officers nodded, wished them a good day, and went off. Tree saw the blue Mercedes Benz coming to a stop at the curb. "There's our ride."

A tall black man with a sharply-angled face framed by shoulder-length dreadlocks got out and waved at them. "Ms. Stayner?" he called.

Freddie waved back and said, "That's me."

The tall man with the dreadlocks wore a gold ring in his left ear, and he was dressed in a dark business suit with a white shirt and tie. When Freddie and Tree reached the car, he said, "Hey there. My name is Issac, but everyone, they call me Bad Boy."

"Funny," Tree said. "Where I come from, that's what they call me."

Bad Boy broke into a smile. "Two bad boys together. Look out world!" He held the door open for them. "Mr. Hale, he's waiting for you."

"This should be interesting," Freddie said.

Contact Ron:

ronbase@ronbase.com
ronbase.wordpress.com
ronbase.com
Check out The Sanibel Sunset Detective Facebook page

CPSIA information can be obtained at www.ICGtesting.com
Printed in the USA
LVOW11s1221260116

472275LV00001B/1/P